TIME TO KILL

DI SARA RAMSEY
BOOK SEVENTEEN

M A COMLEY

ACKNOWLEDGMENTS

Special thanks as always go to @studioenp for their superb cover design expertise.

My heartfelt thanks go to my wonderful editor Emmy, and my proofreaders Joseph and Barbara for spotting all the lingering nits.

Thank you also to my amazing ARC Group who help to keep me sane during this process.

To Mary, gone, but never forgotten. I hope you found the peace you were searching for my dear friend. I miss you each and every day.

ALSO BY M A COMLEY

PROLOGUE

$\mathcal{W}$atching and, more importantly, waiting, was the name of the game for him this evening. He had dutifully followed the target for the past week, and tonight was the night he would make his move. Grinning, he settled into his seat and pulled the cap over his eyes. He could afford to have at least a thirty-minute snooze. His target would be at his designated location for the next couple of hours, what with him being a creature of habit and all.

He dropped off instantly. His snooze was filled with moments that had taken place over the past few months and ended with the expectation of the events that were about to come in the days and weeks ahead of him. Stirring, Owen tipped his cap back and adjusted his position. He glanced around the interior of the car, highlighted by the light from the nearby lamppost, and grinned again, delighted with his acquisition. He had his wits about him. Everything would go according to plan, he'd ensure it would. Every last detail had been meticulously planned with one purpose in mind: to evade capture.

There were those he had crossed paths with over the

years who had slated him for being sloppy. Although he hadn't thought it at the time, they had been right in their assumption. No longer, though. He'd spent the last nine months smartening up his act, becoming a force to be reckoned with. The cops wouldn't know what hit them once it all kicked off. He was prepared for the onslaught that was to come. Forward planning was the ultimate key to success, and he was determined to come away from this mission victorious.

He switched on the radio and tapped along to an old Duran Duran song that he'd detested when it had first been released. *It's taken a while, but I've finally changed for the better. Grown in confidence. Now I appreciate my capabilities and no longer doubt them, like others have in the not-too-distant past. I'm ready... bring it on.*

All he needed to do now was hang on to his patience. That was the one downside he could think about that might get in the way. His patience had always got the better of him in the past. Although he'd worked rigorously on it lately, it was still a niggling doubt in his mind whether he would be able to combat the issue, if it arose. He sucked in a large breath and let it out slowly. After watching some self-help clips on YouTube, he was sure he'd conquered how to control his breathing enough to make a difference to the anger that rippled beneath the surface. It was that he needed to control more than anything else.

The door to the pub opened, and a couple staggered out. The man had his arm looped over the woman's shoulders and he pulled her in for a drunken kiss at the top of the steps. He could tell they were both plastered and unaware of what was going on around them. They tripped down the first step and righted themselves in a fit of giggles. He thought how easy it would be to swoop and kill them both but then reprimanded himself—they weren't his target. Why waste his energy and skills on strangers? Individuals not worthy of his ability?

Another half an hour dragged past. His breathing came in ebbs and flows. His impatience had threatened to surface now and again but, so far, he'd managed to restrain it by concentrating on his breathing, clenching and unclenching his fists in time to the music, delighted by the results he'd managed to achieve so far.

Now all he had to do was wait a little while longer for his target to appear. He glanced at the digital clock on the dashboard and nodded. Not long now, ten minutes tops. The door to the pub swung open a second time, and his gaze was drawn to a man leaving and making his way down the steps towards his car. *How irresponsible of people to go to the pub for a few bevvies only to drive home afterwards. Is it any wonder they have accidents and possibly take innocent people's lives? Selfish bastards.*

Again, he reprimanded himself for going over the top with his thinking. Maybe he was doing the guy an injustice. He hadn't come out of the pub inebriated, unlike the couple who had left before him. Maybe he'd only consumed soft drinks during his time inside.

His gaze was drawn back to the pub's entrance. The door opened a third time. His pulse raced; Ben was finally leaving. He knew the man usually walked home from the pub, or should that be staggered? Either way, he waited until Ben got to around ten feet ahead of him before he left the car. He removed the black holdall from the boot then set off on foot after him.

Ben turned the next corner, giving him the chance to speed up and gain the advantage. Poking his head around the fence panel that led up the alley, he paused and tutted as Ben relieved himself up one of the panels.

His gaze drifted the length of the alley. His surveillance

3

had revealed that it wasn't used much at this time of the day, although it was a busy thoroughfare during daylight hours. That's why he'd deliberately chosen this location, because he knew the body of his victim would be discovered at first light. A biting wind whipped around him. He combatted it by rearranging the collar of his jacket. He paused for a moment and then made his move once Ben had shaken the drips off his todger and zipped up his trousers. Ben took a few steps but toppled into the fence panel on his right. He lashed out and swore at the offending inanimate object and continued on his journey.

He bided his time, waited until Ben was far enough away from the streetlight, then pounced. He shoulder charged Ben into the fence. Ben swore at him, his words slurring, and he tried to right himself, but his coordination was way off the mark. His hand slipped several times, and his legs gave way beneath him.

He lowered his head to the victim's, resting his forehead against his. He nudged it a few times. "Get up, moron."

"Who are you? What do you want? Why don't you just sod off, be on your way and leave me alone?"

"Get up. Stop asking dumb questions and get to your feet."

"I can't," Ben slurred. "You're going to have to help me."

He tore open the zipper of his holdall and, after snapping on a pair of gloves, located the item he was searching for. "Okay, you asked for help, I'm going to give it to you."

"Gee, thanks, that's good of ya."

He took Ben's right arm and placed it against the fence above his head then fired the weapon. The two-inch nail passed through Ben's palm with ease. Shocked, Ben screamed. Before Ben had the chance to realise what was about to happen next, he quickly grabbed Ben's other arm. He held the nail gun up against his palm, pinning it to the fence panel. Again, Ben cried out. He kicked himself for slipping up and shoved a hand into his bag to retrieve a wad of cloth which he forced into Ben's mouth. Was it too little too late? Craning an ear for any sign of movement, he let out a relieved sigh when silence finally descended. The only sounds swirling around him were those of the fierce wind and the discarded leaves from the nearby trees.

Ben's eyes widened. There was a fleeting recognition in their depths.

He smiled. "You know me, don't you?"

Ben nodded and attempted to kick out. No contact was made because he had minimal control over his limbs. Drink had the knack of numbing a person's abilities. If only people realised how vulnerable they became with the demon liquid inside them.

"That was silly. Now your punishment is going to be ten times worse."

Tears emerged and dripped onto Ben's cheeks. He shook his head and glanced sideways at his right arm. Sickened by seeing himself pinned to the fence, he said something, but the cloth muffled his words.

"What? You're not happy with what I've done to you so far? Too bad. That's just the beginning, mate. You wait until I've had a bit more fun with you, you'll be begging me to end your life in a few minutes."

Ben's gaze followed his hand to the bag once more. This time he withdrew a set of pliers. Ben's eyes widened, and he vigorously shook his head. He said something indecipherable, probably pleading with him not to go through with his intentions. No fear of that happening. Owen was on course to end this fucker's life, and he'd take pleasure in making him suffer in the process.

Owen reached up for Ben's right hand, and as he removed each of his fingernails, Ben let out a muffled scream with each fingernail torn from his hand. What was the point in attempting to get free when he was pinned in place? *Some people really are as thick as shit when they find themselves backed into a corner. Idiot. You shouldn't have downed so many pints this evening, then you wouldn't be in this situation, would you, chum? Dense, that's what you are, denser than the thickest part of the Amazon rainforest.*

With the task completed, he moved on to the left hand and did the same, discarding the fingernails on the ground each side of the victim. The cloth served its purpose by deadening Ben's cries for help. By now, he was a snivelling wreck. Snot mixed with the tears streaming down his flushed cheeks.

"Had enough yet? You can die when you want, I don't give a shit if you go early, although I'd prefer it if you stuck around to see what else I have in store for you."

Ben's head twisted from one side to the other, and yet another muffled plea was forced back by the gag.

He laughed, removed a hacksaw from the holdall and ran his hand up and down the handle.

By now, Ben's eyes were bulging, almost popping out of their sockets. He watched the blade get closer to the fingers on his right hand. He kicked out with his legs again; this time they made contact, but the attempt proved pointless. It didn't prevent the hacksaw connecting with the little finger and slicing through it until it was hanging by a thread of skin. Ben coughed as though choking on the rising bile. The next finger was a tad harder, and the next one after that as well. But the hardest joint to get through belonged to Ben's thumb. Ben attempted to shout, to kick his assailant, but nothing would prevent the attack from reaching its ultimate conclusion.

Owen continued on to the next hand and did the same, leaving all the digits hanging by sinews and skin. The colour had drained from Ben's cheeks. "Had enough yet? You're on the verge of passing out, I can sense it. It's okay, I won't allow that to happen. I'll wake you up. I wouldn't want you to miss out on anything important." Next, he unzipped the man's jeans and pulled out his penis.

Ben thrashed, or tried to, but Owen sat across Ben's legs and with the nails embedded in his hands, he knew he wouldn't be going anywhere soon. Ben squirmed, frustrated.

After locating the man's shrivelled member, Owen flopped it out of the zip and placed the teeth of the saw against the skin. Ben passed out. He slapped his face hard to wake him up, determined Ben should see what was about to become of his manhood. It was easy to see the sheer terror in Ben's eyes. Should he wriggle, try to get free, or stay still and take his punishment?

He tipped his head back and laughed. "You're going to enjoy this, having a different set of teeth around it, other than Tess's, for a change."

Another muffled plea for help fell on deaf ears. Holding Ben's penis upright, Owen sawed at the bottom until Ben's member was free. Ben continually writhed and cried out, but his inept movements did nothing to avoid the inevitable. Ben stared at his penis being held up in front of him, and then his gaze dropped to the blood spurting out of the open wound. His head lolled to the side. He'd passed out for a second time, but Owen wasn't finished with this dirtbag yet, not by a long shot. A bottle of water aimed at Ben's face soon brought him around.

"I warned you what would happen if you passed out on me." He reached into his holdall once more and removed a claw hammer. After tapping it a couple of times on his palm, he located Ben's right knee in the dark and smashed it.

Ben screamed and rested his head against the fence panel, swishing it from side to side in an attempt to combat the

7

pain. The hammer located its next target, Ben's other knee, then it moved on to both of his shins and his ankles. Ben's cries for help became weaker. Owen knew Ben was on his way out. He took the hammer and held it up in front of his victim's eyes. Taunting him. Ben was mesmerised by the implement, traumatised by what was in store for him.

The hammer swung towards him and made contact with his temple, not once, twice, or even three times. The blows built in intensity until Ben's head finally hung loose.

Owen felt his victim's pulse—there wasn't one. It was time to pack up his bag and leave. A job well done. One of many to come. He had a list to go through and he would take pleasure ticking the names off, one by one, until he reached the end.

Let the games begin!

CHAPTER 1

 I Sara Ramsey had a feeling today was going to be one of those days. Her cat, Misty, had been sick during the night and had left deposits of vomit littered throughout the downstairs of the house. Her husband, Mark, had told Sara to go off to work and leave the clearing up for him to do, but she had declined his offer. His schedule was as equally punishing as hers, and Misty was her cat, her responsibility. Being a vet, Mark had checked Misty over and determined that she was fit and well. Apart from the vomiting, she didn't have a temperature or any other symptoms that concerned him. He promised Sara that he would nip home during his lunch hour to check on Misty. So Sara had insisted the clean-up should be something she embarked upon herself.

Not the most pleasant of chores in this world, but needs must. She had hugged Misty gently before leaving the house. Surprisingly, Misty had wriggled out of her arms to get free, whereas normally, she enjoyed her snuggles with Sara.

Because of the unexpected delay at home, Sara got snared up in the traffic heading into the city of Hereford. Instead of allowing the situation to overwhelm her, she switched on the radio and flicked through the stations until a song she liked took her fancy. It wasn't long before she was drumming to the beat of an old Lionel Richie song, "Dancing on the Ceiling". Jigging along to the music, she couldn't help wondering what would turn up on her desk that day. It had been a few weeks since a complex investigation had come her way and, while she had enjoyed the reprieve, now she was ready and waiting to sink her teeth into a case that would tax her brain and keep her on her toes. Although, when that happened, it generally meant that someone had lost their life. Maybe she should rethink what she wished for in her working life.

The station appeared on the horizon and, she drew into the car park. She noticed her partner's car was missing from its usual spot and wondered if everything was okay with Carla. Sara collected her bag and phone from the passenger seat and left the car. She'd almost made it to the entrance when Carla's car pulled in.

Sara delayed her entrance and waited for her partner to join her. "Everything all right? You seem as harassed as I was when I got up this morning."

Carla frowned. "Oh, why? I mean, why were you harassed?"

"Lots of cat's puke to deal with. Come on, what's your problem?"

"Eww... that's vile. No wonder I've decided to steer clear of having a pet."

Sara waved a hand. "Part and parcel of having a fur baby, I'd be lost without her. You're avoiding my question, what's up?"

"Nothing, apart from me running late this morning."

Sara glanced behind Carla. Des's car drew into a nearby space. "Ah, it wouldn't have anything to do with Des just arriving and looking equally harassed, would it?"

"Nothing wrong with your detective skills, DI Ramsey. Would you mind if we leave it there for now?"

"Sure. Are you two all right?"

Carla sighed and rolled her eyes. "I asked you to leave it. I need to get inside."

Sara stepped aside and shouted, "Morning, Des. Nice morning."

"I suppose so," came his terse response.

Sara took that as her cue to enter the main building. Carla had already left the reception area and gone upstairs.

"Morning, ma'am. How are you today?" Jeff, the amiable desk sergeant, asked with his normal cheery smile.

"I'm fine. And you, Jeff?"

"Fair to middling, ma'am, I can't complain, unlike some around here." He raised an eyebrow and gestured with his head at the inner door.

Sara knew he was referring to her partner. She pointed behind her. "There's another one on his way." She put a finger to her lips and winked. "Seems like a lovers' tiff to me. I'm out of here."

"Ah, I'm with you. I hope your day improves."

"So do I, Jeff. See you later."

The outer door opened and slammed shut again after Des walked through it. Sara didn't bother hanging around to find out what was going on. Instead, she punched in her code and entered the inner sanctum of the station, leaving the door open for Des to follow her.

Sara jogged up the stairs only for a waft of air to swirl beside her as Des sprinted past her. She was wise enough to know when to keep quiet. She took a quick detour and stopped off at the ladies' toilets. One of the cubicles was closed. She strained an ear to hear the faint sound of sniffling and then someone blowing their nose.

"Carla, is that you?"

A slight pause followed, another sniffle, and finally the toilet flushed. Sara folded her arms and leant against the sink until the door to the cubicle opened. A watery-eyed and rosy-cheeked Carla emerged and walked towards her.

"I'm all right, don't make a fuss," she pleaded.

"Make a fuss? Aren't I allowed to be concerned about you? There's obviously something either on your mind or getting you down, sweetheart. I'm here if you need to chat, any time of the day."

"I know. I just needed to have a good cry to get it out of my system. I feel better already."

Sara smiled and rubbed Carla's arm. "Have you two fallen out? Or is that the dumbest question I've ever asked?"

A glimmer of a smile appeared, and Carla took up the challenge of repairing the damage her mini-breakdown had caused to her makeup. "It's something and nothing."

Sara faced the mirror and studied her partner. "About the wedding, I take it?"

"Why does it all have to be so stressful? At first everything seemed to be a joy to deal with, but recently the venue, caterers, the bridal shop have conspired together to make my life a living hell the last couple of weeks. I'm fed up with chasing my tail, compromising on what plans we put in place months ago."

Sara shrugged. "You know my thoughts on having a big do, don't you? Don't! Take yourself off up to Gretna Green and tie the knot up there with two witnesses loitering aimlessly outside."

Carla gasped. "Like that's going to solve anything. Actually, it'll only make matters worse, won't it?"

"Not at all. There are two people who matter here, you and Des. Or are you telling me the strain is that excessive, you've fallen out of love with him?"

Carla held her gaze in the mirror for a few seconds and then went back to fixing her makeup.

"Shit! Have you, Carla?"

Her partner let out a sigh and puffed out her cheeks. "Honestly? I don't know," she whispered.

"Damn and shit. It's imperative you talk about it. Ignoring each other or being angry with one another is only going to exacerbate the situation."

"Tell *him* that. I tried to speak to him last night, and he raised a hand…"

Sara gasped and yanked on Carla's arm, forcing her to face her. "What? He hit you?"

Carla shook her head and tutted. "If you'll let me finish. I was going to say he raised a hand, putting a halt to the discussion."

"Phew, I thought you were going to tell me that he lashed out at you."

"Your suspicious mind will get you into bother one of these days." Carla chuckled.

"Sorry. I should have more faith in you. I know deep down you would never put up with that shit again. You're much tougher these days, aren't you?"

"Too bloody right I am. Maybe I need to just start putting my foot down in our relationship, see where that leads."

"It's better to make the changes now, love, it'll be a darn sight harder further down the line. Just tell him you want a simple wedding, only you and him at the registry office. Seriously, why go through all this heartache and expense for one day in your life? To hold a wedding that will probably take you ten years to pay off?" Sara held a hand over her heart. "It's what's in here that matters, not how quickly your bank accounts are going to empty to line other folks' pockets. The prices these venues and wedding specialists charge these days are extortionate."

13

"I know you're right, believe me, I do. But what about our parents? It's going to break their hearts and cause a rift between us all if I pull out now and demand that things be done my way."

"I know. It's a tough call. Maybe sitting everyone down and discussing it as a family is the answer. Compromise is definitely the key. Either that or you call the whole thing off. Look at you, I can see how much all of this is tearing you apart, hon. A wedding should be a joyful occasion, not a painful one. I feel for you."

"I know. Maybe it's me going over the top, you know, wanting everything to go smoothly on the road to happiness."

Sara wrinkled her nose. "The road to happiness can often be fraught with unexpected bumps and indecisions, Carla. My advice would be to go away with Des for a few days and lay everything on the table, but first of all, you need to take a step back and see if all this hassle is going to be worth it in the end."

"Meaning?"

"You need to take time out to reassess your relationship, see if all this heartache is worthwhile. I hate to see you in such a state. It's not normal for someone to be in such turmoil and pain when they're planning their own wedding."

Carla gulped and then continued to touch up her eyeshadow. "You're saying I should call it off and go back to being a miserable spinster, is that it?"

Sara raised a pointed finger. "Don't go twisting my words, young lady. I'm simply saying that taking a step back and looking at things from a different angle may help you realise what you have. The relationship was a bit of a whirlwind one, after all, wasn't it?"

"We're not kids, Sara. We're in our early thirties, not teenagers."

"The haze of dealing with a new relationship can be difficult to see through at times. Everything is hunky-dory until something develops and throws a spanner in the works."

"Such as planning a wedding."

"Exactly. You need to figure out if all this upheaval, physical and emotional, will be worth it in the end. All I'm saying is that I hate to see you in tears, distressed and upset. Love should leave you feeling fuzzy inside, not as miserable as fucking sin. There, I've said it. You asked for my opinion, don't go falling out with me now that I've given it."

"I wouldn't. Thank you for being honest with me. I promise this won't affect my work today."

Sara raised her hands. "I didn't think for one minute that it would." Which was a bare-faced lie on her part.

"You go on ahead. I'll finish trying to make myself look more human and be with you shortly."

Sara placed a hand on Carla's back. "In my eyes, you're beautiful inside and out, and no amount of makeup is going to enhance that beauty, so don't go slapping on too much."

"Thank you. You're the best friend a girl could ever hope to have."

"Don't be daft. I'll leave you to it. Coffee?"

"Please. I'll be out in a jiffy."

Sara left the loos and entered the incident room. The rest of the team were all there, sipping coffee and starting their day's work. "Morning all. Everyone okay?"

"Morning, boss," the team responded in unison.

Sara stopped off at the drinks station and fixed Carla and herself a cup of coffee. She glanced up when Carla entered the room and walked towards her. Sara completed the drinks and offered a mug to her partner. "I'll be in my office dealing with the utter dross, I mean the important emails and letters from HQ. Will you guys continue with the tasks I set you yesterday? The sooner we get this backlog of files and paperwork out of the way, the easier our lives are going to be in the immediate future."

"Yeah, I'll lend a hand if anyone needs me," Carla added.

Sara smiled and left them to it. She opened her office door and shuddered. The room was cold. She fiddled with the radiator thermostat, and the water instantly ran through the pipes. After taking in the breathtaking view of the Brecon Beacons in the distance for a few seconds, she continued to her desk, shocked to see how many brown envelopes were sitting in her in-tray. "Jesus, give me a break, for Christ's sake. One of these days I'll turn up for work and have a clear desk at the beginning of the day instead of at the end of it. I live in hope anyway."

"That's the first sign, so they say," Carla said from the doorway.

"What is?"

"Talking to yourself, it's the first sign someone should be locked up."

Sara sat behind her desk and offered up her wrists. "Take me now."

They both laughed.

"You're nuts," Carla said. "I mean that in a kind and caring way, of course."

"I believe you. It's good to see you with a smile on your face. Now bugger off, I have work to do."

"I wanted to drop by and say thanks. There, I've said it, now I'll leave you to it."

"My door is always open for you, no matter how busy I appear to be, Carla."

"I know, and it's appreciated. Do you need a hand?"

"I'll tear them all open and decide then. I'll be in touch if I do."

Carla closed the door behind her on the way out. Sara sighed, picked up her letter opener and sliced through the flap of the first envelope. It was yet another form to fill out from HQ, one that she set aside to deal with later.

After ten minutes, the phone rang, disturbing her concentration. Up until then, she had been on a roll, flying through and dealing with the post like she was on some kind of deadline before all the envelopes tripped an explosion. Maybe her mind was still on the movie she'd watched with Mark over the weekend, *Mission Impossible*.

Setting the envelopes aside, she answered the phone. "DI Sara Rams—"

"It's me. I could do with you attending this one."

Sara rolled her eyes. She knew full well who the caller was, but the devil rose in her. "Sorry, who is this?"

"Screw you, Sara. If you're not interested then I'll find someone who is."

"Hold your horses, Lorraine. Don't get your nylons in a bloody twist."

Her pathologist friend tutted. "In case you hadn't noticed, I live in trousers or one of these damn paper suits. Actually, not forgetting the greens I'm subjected to perform in."

"All right. Fair point. Why do you need my assistance?"

"Did I say that?"

"Oh, touché. You need me to attend, not my assistance, my mistake."

"Can we cut the crap? I'm not in the mood for messing around today, Sara. You need to get here ASAP."

"Where's here?"

"Broomy Hill. Do you know it? Close to the Waterworks Museum."

"I'll be there in fifteen minutes. Sorry for winding you up."

"You're forgiven. It's a bad one."

"Shit! I'm on my way." She ended the call and tucked all the post back into the in-tray; it could wait until later. She left the office. "Carla, we need to get on the road. Lorraine's just called, she's at the scene. It's a bad one, apparently."

"Oh heck." Carla sprang to her feet.

They tore down the main staircase, passing DCI Carol Price who was on her way up to her office.

"Is there a fire?" she asked.

"A bad crime scene. Lorraine has summoned us. I'll fill you in later, gov," Sara shouted over her shoulder.

"Make sure you do. I'm intrigued to know what it's all about."

Sara pushed open the security door and raced past Jeff on the front desk. "Can't stop to chat."

"I wouldn't expect you to, ma'am. Good luck."

"Thanks, Jeff."

"Where are we going?" Carla belted herself into the passenger seat.

Sara pulled away from the station and entered the flow of traffic before she answered. "Broomy Hill, near the Waterworks Museum."

"I know it. It's fairly built up around there. What are we going to discover when we get there, do you know?"

"Nope. Lorraine told me to expect a bad one. She was in a foul mood; just warning you not to wind her up when we get there."

"As if I would. I usually leave that for you to do."

"Well, in that case, I'm prewarning both of us to show some restraint."

THEY ARRIVED AT THE SCENE. There were two patrol cars already in situ and a couple of forensic team vehicles. Lorraine was at the rear of her van, searching for something. She briefly glanced up and waved then got back to what she was doing. Sara and Carla pulled on a protective suit, snapped on a pair of gloves and then went over to say hello, carrying their protective shoe coverings for later use, once they got closer to the scene.

"Hi. How's it going, Lorraine?"

Lorraine peered up at the grey clouds gathering overhead. "It's a race against time, ladies. We've been lucky up until now, the rain has held off, but who knows for how long that's going to be the case?"

Sara followed Lorraine's gaze towards the alley. "I take it a marquee has been erected?"

"In the process of being done now. We had to wait for it to arrive... don't ask. Hence my foul mood."

"Sorry, mate. You can do without the extra hassle when you have a bad one to deal with."

"Tell me about it. Sign the log and meet me down the alley."

A cordon had been set up at the end of the fenced corridor. Sara and Carla flashed their IDs at the uniformed officer, and Sara signed the log. The constable raised the tape high enough for them to duck under. They immediately put the coverings over their shoes, preventing them from contaminating the area.

"Oh fuck, will you look at the state of him," Carla whispered, her eyes drawn to the victim.

"Jesus. He must have gone through hell to end up like that. There's blood everywhere," Sara replied. She inched forward to stand alongside Lorraine. "Care to run through his injuries? Although, I think most of them are clear enough to see."

"Apart from the obvious, that over there," Lorraine pointed at what appeared to be a shrivelled finger lying on the ground off to their right, "is the man's penis."

"Holy shit! Why would someone do that to another human being? It was a rhetorical question, ladies. God, I

19

don't know about you guys, but I can confirm my gag reflexes are in full working order at present. That poor man. This strikes me as personal, right, Lorraine?"

"We've dealt with similar situations before, but this one is different. Don't ask me to explain why, it's just a feeling I have in my gut. We all need to listen to those now and again, don't we?"

"We do. So he was nailed to the fence first?" Sara surmised.

"I think you've nailed that one, Sara. Sorry, poor taste at a time like this. Yes, his fingernails have been ripped out and a few fingers cut off with what appears to be a jagged-edged saw. I'm thinking a hacksaw."

"The blood on his trousers, obviously that came from his penis being cut off, or am I missing something else?" Sara asked. She took a step closer to the victim and crouched.

Lorraine nodded and confirmed, "His shins are busted into pieces, and both his kneecaps are shattered. Oh yes, not to mention each ankle took a hammering as well as his temple."

"Bloody hell. Someone really hated this guy. There's no way this is a random attack. I'm guessing the perpetrator came here prepared, with what looks like a bagful of tools to assist him."

Lorraine applauded Sara's appraisal of the victim's injuries. "I couldn't have put it better myself. I would agree, he was specifically targeted and tortured. Maybe he didn't even get a chance to cry out and ask for help, not with a wad of cloth bunged into his mouth. I'd say the killer was fully equipped and primed for action."

Sara shuddered at the thought. "Bugger. Do you have any ID on the victim?"

"Plenty. If the killer wanted to disguise the victim's ID

then I'm presuming he would have taken his phone and bank cards with him instead of leaving them at the scene."

"Makes our lives easier." Sara glanced around. There was an old man at the end of the alley, talking to a uniformed officer who was taking notes. "Is that the man who discovered the body?"

"Correct. I asked him to hang around. Told him you'd be needing a chat with him. As you can imagine, he's pretty shaken up, so tread carefully."

Sara raised an eyebrow. "As in I don't usually?"

"Sod off. That's not what I was inferring at all, and you know it," Lorraine growled. "I need to get on. The weather is going to be against us soon."

Sara issued a taut smile. "We'll leave you to it and call back after we've spoken to the witness."

"As you will."

Sara and Carla removed their shoe coverings and slipped them into the awaiting black bag, collecting all the protective clothing used by those attending the scene. While Sara walked towards the witness, she cast her eye over him. He paced the area and ran a hand through his greying hair now and then. In between, he played with his goatee.

"He seems agitated before we even get a chance to speak with him," Carla whispered out of the corner of her mouth.

"Glad it's not only me thinking that. Let's see what he has to say and assess the situation afterwards."

"Suits me."

Sara produced her warrant card and held it up for the man to see. "I'm DI Sara Ramsey, and this is my partner, DS Carla Jameson. Sorry, I haven't been made aware of your name, sir."

"Don't be. The woman with the flaming-red hair didn't bother taking it. I'm Donald Kelley."

"And you were the person who found the body, is that correct?"

"Unfortunately, yes. Why did I have to come this way this morning?"

"I take it this isn't your usual route then?"

"That's right. I prefer to vary my journey into town to break the monotony. I come this way maybe twice a week on different days. Why today? Why did I have to be the one to discover him? I feel as sick as a bloody dog. Desperate to get home, I am, but no, I was told I had to wait here for someone senior to arrive. That would be you, would it?"

"It would. I can only apologise for any inconvenience caused. Cases like this are few and far between."

"Who are you trying to bloody kid? I've got eyes and ears. I see and hear what's going on in the news. The state this city is in with the number of serial killers we've got on the loose around here. It's a disgrace, that's what it is. Worse still since the bloody lockdown. All those people with pent-up feelings, venting their sodding anger as soon as the all-clear has been given. Taking out innocent people like that. What a way to go. That ain't normal, the person who did this can't be right in the head, can they? Shocking behaviour. Not sure what this world is coming to from one day to the next. Crimes like this... not only this but all those crimes against the babies, the little children who have lost their lives lately... appalling state of affairs. The bastards need rounding up and hanging, the lot of them. Why let them sit in a cell, allowed to watch TV all day long and being fed three square meals a day?"

Sara and Carla exchanged glances.

Sara sighed. "You have a right to feel aggrieved, sir. As police officers, we're doing our very best to clamp down on crimes of this magnitude, but it's not easy."

"I bet it isn't. You need to get the officers back on the street. Big men, built like brick shithouses like they used to be when I was a kid. They used to scare the crap out of me when one of them came marching around the corner. All the kids scarpered quick smart, they did. Not nowadays. When a patrol car shows up anywhere, you can see the defiance on the kids' faces. Evil fuckers, they are."

"In your opinion, Mr Kelley," Sara interjected quickly.

"Yeah, all right. One that I'm entitled to as well. I've been around the block a few times but I've never seen anything like that. It's a good job I've got a cast-iron stomach. Can I go now? I've been waiting ages for you to show up."

"Soon. I have a few more questions I'd like to ask first. Did you see anyone else in the immediate area?"

His gaze seared into hers. "Nope. You really think I would have stuck around if I had? Next question."

"What about the victim, do you know him?"

"I think I've seen him a few times down at the Flying Horse but I've never stopped and had a chat, if that's what you're asking."

"So you think he might be local?"

"More than likely. He visits the same pub I go to, so I suppose he must be, right? I don't have to be a copper to figure that out now, do I?"

"Thank you, Mr Kelley. If you give us your address, we'll send a police officer around to take a statement from you, if that's okay?"

His mouth gaped open, and he shook his head then said, "Wow, is that it? I've wasted all this time for you to show up and ask a few measly questions, and now you're telling me I can go. There's something wrong with that."

"We can either let you go or we can take you down to the station and hold you as a suspect if you'd rather," Sara said, her patience waning rapidly with the man's terse attitude.

He took a step towards her and pointed at her chest.

"Now wait just a minute. Here I am, trying to do you a favour, and this is how you treat me."

The male officer rushed forward to get in between Sara and the enraged Kelley. "All right, let's give the inspector some space to breathe, sir."

Kelley remained defiant for a few extra seconds and then finally yielded. He ran a hand through his hair and turned away from them. "Sorry." His apology was only just audible. "My address is fifteen Chatsworth Road, just around the corner there. Can I go now?"

"You can. Thank you for waiting around, going out of your way to have a conversation with us, Mr Kelley. An officer will be in touch with you soon."

He turned his back and walked off, mumbling as he went.

"What a rude man," Carla hissed.

Sara stared after him. "Yeah, maybe we should give him a break. It's not every day you stumble across a partially dismembered body lying in an alley."

"I suppose so. We should get on before we get caught in a downpour, I can feel it in the air."

They made their way back to Lorraine and her crew, who were in the process of erecting the marquee.

"Can we lend a hand?" Sara offered, not that she'd have a clue where to start. It was good to offer, though.

"We've got it covered. How did you get on?"

"Didn't get much out of him other than a bloody lecture, you know the type. Although he did tell us the victim is local, or should I say he's presuming he's from around here, because he frequents the same boozer as himself."

"Ah, I can tell he pissed you off. Easily remedied, we've got the victim's ID, so you'll be able to see for yourself." Lorraine swooped down and picked up a plastic evidence bag. "Benjamin Connor, twenty-six Penfold Street."

"Thanks, Lorraine. If you no longer need us, we'd better

get round there and break the news to his relatives, if he lives with anyone, if not, we'll do our best to track down his family by the end of the day."

"Good luck. I'd rather be lumbered with my job today than yours. Shit! Here comes the rain now."

"We're going to make a dash for it. Be in touch soon. Get the report to me when you can, please."

"I'll do my best. Don't forget to shove your suits in the black bag before you leave."

"Don't worry, we won't."

Carla had already stripped off her protective suit and was halfway to the car by the time Sara had finished speaking with Lorraine. Sara's hair stuck to the side of her face as she slipped out of the suit. She shoved it in the bag and bolted for the car as a rumble of thunder shattered the silence surrounding them.

"Jesus, I'm wet through. Didn't anticipate it coming down that quickly." She leant forward and put the heater on to dry her hair. "Do you know Penfold Street?"

"Yeah, it's not too far. I'll tell you which way to go. Take a right at the top of this road."

Sara started the engine and carried out her partner's instructions. A droplet of rain slipped down the back of her blouse, and she quivered. "Damn rain, I hate it."

Carla laughed. "Apart from gardeners and ducks, name me one person who does like it."

"Ha, yeah, silly me. Where to now?"

"Left and then a sharp right."

They drew up outside a mid-terraced house with no front garden.

"Are you ready for this?" Sara asked.

"Not really. I'd rather you did this on your own, but the odds on that happening are negligible, right?"

"Yep. I need your support, matey. Come on, let's get it

over with."

Sara locked the car and dashed the few steps to the front door, pulling her collar up around her neck to prevent more rain dripping down her back. She rang the bell and knocked at the same time, eager to be heard. The door was yanked open within seconds. She offered up her ID to a young blonde woman who was sporting a black eye. "Hi, we're DI Sara Ramsey and DS Carla Jameson. Would you be Mrs Connor?"

"No. We're not married. I'm Ben's girlfriend, Tess Armstrong, we live together." She peered behind Sara and asked, "Where is he? Did he get off his face again?"

"It would be better if we spoke inside, Miss Armstrong."

Tess took a step back behind the door and gestured for them to enter the dark and dingy hallway. The dull day was partially to blame for the bleakness, although the dark wallpaper played its part, too.

"Come through to the lounge."

The woman walked with a limp and winced a few times during the journey.

Once they were inside the small lounge that seemed a little cluttered to Sara's taste, she asked, "Have you been in an accident, Miss Armstrong?"

"It's Tess. Sort of." She avoided eye contact when she replied.

"Care to enlighten us further?"

"Not really. Just tell me why you're here and leave."

They sat, Sara and Carla on the grey fabric sofa and Tess in the small armchair, her head held low.

"When was the last time you spoke to Benjamin?" Sara probed gently.

"It's Ben, he hates being called Benjamin."

"Sorry. Thank you for correcting me."

"Umm... I saw him at around six last night." Her eyes

narrowed, and she ran a hand over her cheek and then her bruised eye.

"I'm just going to come right out and say it, did he do that to you?"

Silence.

"Tess, we need to know. Did Ben hit you?" Sara repeated.

"No. Yes. I mean, no he didn't hit me, he beat me up. Kicked, punched, pulled my hair out..." The tears she'd obviously been holding back fell onto her cheeks. "I'm better than this. I can't take it any more."

"Is it a regular occurrence? Him laying into you like this?"

"Yes. It's getting worse. I haven't got the money to up and leave him, otherwise I would. Has he been arrested? Is that why you're here?"

Sara inhaled a steadying breath and let it seep between her lips. "No. Tess..." She waited until the woman's gaze met hers and then continued, "We have some bad news for you. I'm sorry to have to tell you that Ben's body was found early this morning."

Tess's eyes widened, and she clutched a hand to her heart. "What? Are you telling me he's dead?"

"That's correct. I can't go into detail but what I can tell you is that Ben suffered before he died."

Tess frowned. "I don't understand. How did he die? In an accident? Did he get run over?"

"Unfortunately not. It would appear that someone tortured Ben before they killed him."

"What? This must be some kind of mistake. Why would someone do that to him?"

"We were hoping you might be able to shed some light on that for us."

Her hand flattened over her chest. "How? Why would you think that?"

"Because you're his girlfriend. We need to know if he's

27

been under any duress recently. Has he fallen out with anyone in the past few weeks or months? By what I can tell, he had a violent nature."

"Yes, he was handy with his fists, but like most abusive men, he only had it in him to take his frustrations out on the woman in his life."

Sara and Carla eyed each other and nodded. As Sara knew only too well because Carla had experienced the same with her ex, who was thankfully out of the picture now that Des was on the scene.

Sara turned her attention back to Tess. "We know his sort have cowardly notions where choosing fights with other males are concerned. Has he mentioned anything that could be useful to our investigation?"

Tess paused for a moment to consider the question. "No, we barely spoke. He used to strike out if I asked him what time he would be in for his dinner. I can't believe he's dead." She let out a breath that some might interpret as a relieved sigh, Sara wasn't sure.

"It's hard living with an abusive partner. Were you together long?"

"A couple of years. He took all my money off me a few months after I moved in here. I was caught, trapped with nowhere to go to and no one to help me. I have no family in the area. My parents are both dead, and my brother lives in Australia. I never hear from him, it's been like that since our parents died. I think he blamed me for their deaths."

Sara sat forward and placed her elbows on her thighs. "May I ask why?"

"You know what men are like. They often get the wrong end of the stick, and once their mind is set on something, it's nigh on impossible to shift that idea."

"How did your parents die?"

"They were on holiday in the Alps, travelling on a cable

28

car when one of the wires snapped. Five people died that day, including my parents."

"My condolences, that must have been awful for you."

"It was. More so when my brother decided to accuse me of their deaths."

Sara inclined her head. "I don't understand. How were you to blame when you weren't there?"

"I paid for the holiday. It was an anniversary gift for them, their thirtieth, and it ended in tragedy."

"And your brother took it upon himself to lay the blame at your door and stop speaking to you? Seems a tad harsh to me."

She shrugged. "What can I do about it? He's the bloody-minded sort. I think his wife has tried to reason with him, but he doesn't want to know me. I can't see him changing his mind in the future, either."

"Gosh, that's unbelievable. Going back to what's happened to Ben, have you seen anyone hanging around the house at all?"

"No, not that I've been looking for anyone. Do you think he was specifically targeted, is that what you're telling me?"

"Possibly. The ferociousness of the attack would indicate that to be the case."

"Oh my. No, I can't think of anything right now, although this has come as a shock to me and I'm possibly not thinking straight at this moment."

"I can understand. Does Ben have any relatives living in the area?"

"Yes, his parents live out at Aconbury. I can give you their address, if you want it?"

"Thanks, that would be great."

Tess left her seat and picked up her handbag from the other side of the room. She removed her phone and scrolled through her contacts. "Here you go." She angled the phone

29

towards Carla who jotted down the address in her notebook.

"Thanks, that's great," Carla said.

"It's the least I can do. I wish I could be of more use to you. What happens now? I've never been in this situation before. I've seen lots of dramas on TV but I'm not sure how accurate they are."

"Pretty accurate. We'll pass on your details to the patholo-gist; she'll be in touch soon. She'll probably need you to ID the body, although looking at the photos dotted around of the two of you together, and the fact his ID was found on his person at the scene, she might agree to scrub round that, unless you want to see him."

Tess closed her eyes, and her shoulders shook. "I couldn't. I've never seen a dead body before. I wonder if his parents will do it."

"I'm sure they will. I don't think it's something you need to stress over. Where did Ben work?"

"In the sports shop in town. He was the assistant manager there. His boss has recently enrolled him in the management scheme."

"I see. The name of the shop?"

"Sporting Chance. I know, dumb name."

Sara smiled. "One last question before we leave."

Tess glanced her way and nodded. "Go on."

"Are you going to be all right? I can call someone to come and sit with you if you like."

"No," Tess was quick to shoot her down. "I've taken a few days off work until the bruises go down and I'm steering clear of my friends for the time being. I don't want to hear people's opinions of what I should do for the best. Their well-intended advice ticks me off. Everyone has a point of view, but if someone has never been in my situation, they have no right to judge or offer advice."

"If you're sure?"

"I am. Is there anything else?"

"No, not right now. We might have to come back to see you if some evidence comes our way that needs clarifying."

"Is that likely?"

"We don't know. Are you okay?"

"I think so. My head is spinning, and my emotions are raw, but I'm sure I'll be fine."

"We'll be off then, as long as you're sure."

"Thank you for your concern."

They all rose from their seats and left the lounge.

At the front door, Sara gave Tess her business card. "Call me if you need to have a chat."

"Thank you, you're very kind."

They ran back to the car to avoid getting another soaking. Tess didn't dawdle at the door, she slammed it shut as soon as they left the threshold.

"Bloody vile day," Carla cursed.

"Yep. I suppose winter is truly with us now, so all we can do is accept it. What did you make of her?"

Carla faced her. "I'm undecided. Why didn't you push things with her?"

"Ah, you noticed I held back. I wanted to get a different take on their relationship before I went any further."

"What are you saying, that you think she's behind Ben's murder?"

"Possibly. Hard to tell. Put yourself in her shoes. She seemed relieved to hear that he was dead, didn't she?"

"I am putting myself in her shoes. Having been in a similar situation, I'd be relieved if my abuser met a gruesome end. However, I doubt if I would have had the courage to have ended his life, though."

"I hear you but I also think we need to keep an open mind on that, just in case."

Carla let out a sigh of her own and leant back against the headrest. "I'll tell you one thing."

"What's that?" Sara turned the key in the ignition and pulled away from the kerb.

"It made me revisit my time with my ex and also made me realise how much I love Des."

"Good. I was hoping you'd say something along those lines. Getting married is one of the most stressful times in our lives, Carla. I would make it as simple as you can. The day is about you two, ignore everything else, nothing else matters, only what is going on in your hearts." Carla wiped away a tear. "Hey, I didn't mean to upset you."

"You haven't. It's me being silly. You're right. I'll discuss it with Des tonight. I just hope it doesn't escalate into an argument again."

"Don't let it. In my experience, you have to learn there are different ways of speaking to your partner to achieve your aims."

"Thanks for the insight. I'm sure we can come to an agreement if we sit down and discuss things, like adults."

"There you go, always think positively even when faced with a bunch of negative scenarios."

"And that's why you're a DI and I'm a DS, is that what you're going to say next?"

Sara laughed. "There's no need to. I will say one thing… don't ever think you're alone. I'm always at the end of the phone day or night, you hear me?"

"I do. Thanks, boss."

"I'm your friend as well as your boss, don't ever forget that either. You and Des were meant to be. I'm sure you'll overcome any obstacles that are likely come your way down the line. My advice would be to look up some breathing exercises to help you combat the stress. They really do help, you know."

"I'll take a look later. Thanks, Sara, you're a force to be reckoned with."

THE HOUSE WAS DETACHED with a large garden at the front, surrounded by similar properties, probably built around fifty years ago, not that Sara was an expert on older properties. She switched off the engine, and the wipers stopped midway across the windscreen. "Great, it's still pouring down. Are you ready to get another soaking?"

"If I must. Someone up there is obviously vexed about something today."

"Yeah, I'm getting that way myself with this bloody weather. Let's hope someone is home."

They exited the car and rushed past a silver Mercedes parked on the road just outside the property which lacked a driveway or a garage.

Sara rang the bell, thankful there was a slight porch for them to shelter under while they waited. It took a few moments, but the door was eventually opened by a lady in her early sixties. She had half-rimmed specs on the tip of her nose which she removed as she spoke.

"Hello. May I help you?"

Sara and Carla both flashed the IDs they were holding.

"Mrs Connor, would it be possible to come in for a chat with you?" Sara asked.

"The police? Regarding what, may I ask?"

"It's about your son."

"Benjamin? Has he done something wrong?"

Sara took a brief look at the weather behind her and smiled at the woman. "It would be better if we spoke inside."

"Of course. I'm so sorry, where are my manners? I'm flummoxed by why you're here. Do come in. Would you like a drink? Tea or coffee?"

"Not for us, thank you. Would you like us to remove our shoes?"

"If you wouldn't mind. Thank you for being so considerate, not many visitors are these days. Come through to the lounge."

After slipping off their shoes and leaving them by the front door, Sara and Carla followed the woman through the large hallway and into a lounge with high ceilings and wooden panelling on the walls. A large gilt mirror decorated the fireplace above a small wood-burning stove. Sara instantly felt comfortable in her surroundings.

"Please, take a seat."

Sara gulped, preparing herself for the announcement that had settled on the tip of her tongue, and sat on the sofa next to Carla. Mrs Connor sat in the Queen Anne chair closest to the fire. She placed her spectacles on the side table next to her and interlocked her fingers in her lap.

"I'm sorry, Mrs Connor, we're here to share some bad news with you," Sara said.

Mrs Connor frowned and inclined her head to the side.

Sara continued, "This morning, we believe we discovered the body of your son, Benjamin Connor. Regrettably, he has been murdered."

Mrs Connor stared at Sara in shock and then covered her face to suppress the sob that emerged. Her head shook over and over, but she didn't say anything until the sob subsided and her hands slipped into her lap again. She glanced sideways and removed a tissue from the box next to her spectacles.

"I'm sorry. This is too much to bear. Would it be possible for you to ring my husband for me?"

"Of course, can you give me his number?"

She removed her mobile from the table, scrolled through

her contact list and handed the phone to Sara. "He should answer within a few rings."

"Is he at work?"

"Yes. He works at the local school, he's a teacher."

The phone rang a few times before the call was diverted to voicemail. "Shall I leave a message?"

She nodded. "Tell him to call me when convenient, please."

Sara relayed the message and then ended the call. "Hopefully your husband will get back to you soon. Is there anyone else I can call in the meantime?"

Mrs Connor stared at the photo on the mantlepiece of her and her husband and shook her head. "No, we're very private people. I don't want anyone else knowing our business. How did Ben die?" she finally asked.

"I'm afraid it wasn't pleasant. It would appear that he was tortured before he was killed."

She gasped. "Why and who would do such a thing? Have you caught the person responsible?"

"Not yet. Someone found your son on their way to work this morning. He was in an alley quite close to his home. The pathologist and SOCO are at the scene now."

"What was he doing in an alley?"

"We called at his home and spoke to Tess. She told us he hadn't been home all night. She was the one who gave us your address."

"Oh, her. And she didn't think to call me? Never mind, it doesn't surprise me in the slightest."

Sara's interest piqued. "Are you saying you don't get along with Tess?"

"I would imagine very few people do," Mrs Connor replied tersely.

"May I ask why?"

"She's a liar. I wouldn't trust her as far as I could throw her."

"Care to tell us more?" Sara asked. She wondered if the woman knew that her son was abusing his girlfriend or not.

"I saw some bruises on her a few months back, asked her if she'd had an accident, and she broke down in tears then blurted out that Ben had hit her. Born liar. My son would never be so cruel as to lay a hand on a woman. I can't be doing with people who make up stories, condemning someone's good name like that. Shame on her."

Sara drew in a large breath. "Well, I have to tell you when we showed up at the house earlier, Tess had a black eye and was wincing as she walked. When I asked what had happened to her, she told us that Ben had beaten her up."

"And you believed her? You need your head read if you do."

"The evidence was pretty clear for us both to see, Mrs Connor."

"Evidence? A few bruises that could have been given to her by anyone or…"

"Or, you think she may have given herself the black eye, is that what you were about to say?"

"Yes. I wouldn't put it past her. You don't know her like I do. She's what I would call an attention seeker."

Sara ran a hand across her brow, unsure what to believe for the best. "Maybe we should leave things there for now, the conversation has been side-tracked a little. The reason we're here is to ask you if you know why anyone would want to hurt your son, Mrs Connor. Did he confide in you?"

"We had very few secrets, we're a close family, and no, he didn't tell me that he'd fallen out with anyone enough for them to want to kill him. This is unthinkable. Are you telling me that you believe my son was intentionally targeted?"

"We're not totally certain at this stage, but the pathologist believes that the injuries show signs that the victim was known to the killer."

"What? How can you possibly tell that? Do you have some kind of crystal ball?"

"No. It's the ferocity of the attack the pathologist goes by..." Sara cringed, mindful that she shouldn't have revealed that fact, but it was too late, it was out in the open now.

Mrs Connor shook her head in disbelief. "What are you saying? Tell me, I want to know the details."

"I can't go into detail, not yet, Mrs Connor, not until we have the post-mortem results which should come through in the next few days."

"I want to see him. Take me to him."

Sara sighed. "As I told Tess, I don't believe the pathologist will call for either of you to ID his body, his ID was found at the scene. But we can't stop you from seeing him, if that's what you want."

Mrs Connor covered her face with her hands and broke down again. Sara's sympathy grew for the poor woman and, distracted, she jumped when Mrs Connor's mobile rang beside her.

"Do you want me to answer it?" Sara asked.

Mrs Connor sniffled and wiped her eyes and then blew her nose on the tissue. "It'll be Richard, he usually calls me back pretty quickly if I leave a message."

Sara answered the phone. "Hello?"

"Joan, what's wrong? You sound strange."

"Is that Mr Connor?"

"Yes, who are you, and what the hell are you doing answering my wife's phone? Where is she? Answer me, damn you."

"I will if you give me a chance, sir. I'm DI Sara Ramsey. I'm at the house with your wife. Is it possible for you to come home?"

"I'm in the middle of teaching a lesson, no, it's not. Is she all right? Why are you at my home?" His voice rose the more questions he asked.

"We came to share some bad news, sir. It would be best if you came home and we can discuss it further when you get here."

"What sort of bad news?"

"Richard, come home, please," Mrs Connor shouted from the other side of the room.

"All right. I'll get someone to cover for me and be there in fifteen minutes at the latest."

"Very well, sir. See you soon." Sara jabbed the End Call button and placed the phone on the sofa between her and Carla. "He's on his way."

"Thank God. I'm warning you, he'll be livid when he gets here."

Sara issued a half-smile. "We're used to people being angry with us for doing our job."

Mrs Connor bowed her head. "I wish I had a cigarette."

"Sorry, neither of us smokes," Sara replied.

"I used to. I gave up fifteen years ago. Maybe I can have a tot of brandy, or would you think badly of me drinking alcohol at this time of the morning?"

"Not at all. You must do whatever eases your pain. Can I get it for you?"

"No, thank you. It'd be easier to get it myself." She left her seat and made her way to the back of the room to a large sideboard where she half-filled a tumbler with brandy. She left the bottle on the top of the cabinet and returned to her seat where she took a sip. "It hasn't helped numb the pain. I thought it would, but I was mistaken."

"Give it time, I'm sure it will help."

The room fell silent until Mrs Connor found her voice again. "My husband should be home soon. He'll demand all sorts when he gets here. I'm going to apologise for his behaviour before he arrives."

"Honestly, there's no need. We're used to grief taking its toll on people in different ways."

A few minutes later, the front door slammed and the lounge door burst open. "Right, what's this all about?"

"Hello, Mr Connor. I'm DI Ramsey, we spoke on the phone earlier. Won't you take a seat?"

"I'm all right standing. Get on with it. Why are you here?"

Sara took in the man's smart appearance, his thinning hair tucked just above his pristine white collar. He removed his grey suit jacket and placed it over the back of the spare armchair.

"Very well. We came to share the sad news that your son's body was found this morning."

The colour drained from his flushed cheeks as if someone had thrown a bucket of ice-cold water over him. "What? Is this true?" he turned to ask his wife.

Mrs Connor reached for her husband's hand and stated in a strained voice, "Yes, Richard, it's true. Someone tortured and killed him."

He released his wife's hand and collapsed into the armchair. "Who did it? Have you caught the bastard yet?"

"Not yet. We were only alerted to the fact your son had passed away first thing this morning. Our priority at this stage is to inform the family before it hits the news headlines."

"I see. Right, you've done that now, you should be going. I want the person who did this punished, and quickly."

"I assure you, so do we. First, we need to get clued up on any background information you can share with us regarding your son."

"Such as?"

39

"If he's had any grievances with someone he knew lately," Sara replied.

"What are you saying, that someone he knew did this to him?"

"Possibly. By what the pathologist has surmised so far, in the limited time she has spent at the crime scene."

"Stop the gobbledegook. I want the facts without you pussyfooting around. How was he killed?"

"We won't be able to establish that fact until the post-mortem has been concluded." *That's all you need to know right now.*

"When will that be?"

"Either later today or tomorrow. The pathologist is very efficient and the best in the business."

"Are we supposed to be reassured by that statement, Inspector?"

"I had hoped it would give you a source of comfort, Mr Connor."

"It doesn't. Our son is dead. In my opinion, that is nothing to be taken lightly. Granted, you must be desensitised to victims losing their lives in your line of business, but we're talking about our only child here. Our treasured son," he said harshly.

"Richard, there's no need for you to be rude," his wife said. "It's not their fault our son is… no longer with us."

"I'm not going to apologise. The pain is immeasurable. I'm hurting and I want answers."

Sara nodded. "Which is your right as a parent, sir. However, the evidence is very thin on the ground at this stage in the investigation. I'm going to need you to bear with us at the moment. I want to assure you that my team is very proficient."

"We are the fortunate ones, aren't we? To have the best of everything, an absolute professional cutting open our son and to have the most outstanding officers the force has to offer on the case to boot," he bit back swiftly.

"Richard, please. You're only making this worse for all of us."

His face clouded over with anger. "Worse? How is that even possible, Joan? Our only child is dead. How could things possibly be worse than learning that?"

His wife put her drink down, dipped her chin to her chest and concealed her head with her hands. She sobbed openly, and for the briefest of moments, her husband did nothing but stare at her.

Sara was horrified by his selfish behaviour and went to stand, only for Mr Connor to stretch out his arm and say, "Stay there, I'll deal with her." He crossed the room and knelt beside his wife. She flung her arms around his neck.

"I don't want all this aggro, Richard. Why can't you accept he's gone and talk to the officers nicely? I repeat, it's not their fault, and here you are treating them like dirt."

Her husband pulled out of her grasp and sat back on his heels. "I'm sorry. It's the shock." He peered over his shoulder at Sara and said, "Please forgive me."

Sara smiled. "There's nothing to forgive, Mr Connor. Is there anything else you can tell us about Ben that you think might be helpful in our investigation?"

He covered his eyes with his hand and shook his head, then said, "No, I can't think of anything. Does his girlfriend know?"

"Yes, we called round to see Tess first as that was the only form of contact we found on your son. She then gave us your address, and we came straight here to break the news."

"And what did she have to say about his death?" His tone had turned harsh once more.

Here we go again! "She was shocked by the news." Sara felt it best not to reveal that she thought the young woman had been relieved to hear the news.

"It'll be an act, knowing her."

"What makes you say that, sir?"

"She knows how to manipulate people, that one. A liar through and through, you mark my bloody words."

"I take it you don't get along?"

"No. We used to, she started off fine until the barriers dropped and her true colours were revealed. But we tolerated her for the sake of our son, he loved her."

"And what about the abuse aspect of their relationship? And yes, we've seen the evidence for ourselves today. Tess had a black eye and had sustained other injuries allegedly caused by your son."

"You only have her word on that, don't you? See, she's fooled you already into believing her vile stories. Don't believe everything that tumbles out of that girl's mouth, I'm imploring you."

"Thank you for the warning. Is there anything else we should know?"

"Isn't that enough?" he replied in an instant, getting to his feet and shaking out his legs. "Damn knees, I should never have got down there in the first place. Is that it? Are we done now? Only I'd like to spend some time alone with my wife before I head back to work."

"You can't go back," Mrs Connor screeched. "I need you here with me."

"All right. I'll ring Mr Robinson, make him aware of the situation. I'll do it in the kitchen. You can show yourselves out, can't you, ladies?"

"Yes. Thank you for speaking with us, Mr Connor. Take care of yourself and your wife. We'll be in touch if we have any news for you."

"I should think so. Goodbye." With that, he marched out of the room, and Mrs Connor burst into tears again.

Sara felt bad for leaving her with the uncaring man at such a distressing time. "Are you sure you're going to be all right, Mrs Connor?"

"Yes. He might come across as a misery guts, but his heart is in the right place, once you get to know him."

"I'm sure. How long have you been married?"

"Thirty-five years next week. We were due to go out for a nice meal with Ben and Tess."

"That's such a shame."

"Now I'll have his funeral to sort out, won't I?"

"It depends on how the post-mortem and the inquiry go. There's a possibility there might be a delay releasing the body."

"Oh no. It's not something I had considered, I just presumed we'd be able to bury him as soon as the post-mortem had been carried out."

"I'll have a word with the pathologist and get back to you later, if that's okay?"

"Thank you for your kindness. I feel comfortable with you handling the case, Inspector."

"That's good to hear. We'll be going then. We're going to drop by Ben's work now, see if his colleagues can add anything worth delving into."

"Wishing you every success. I want the person who did this found. They shouldn't be allowed to get away with killing Ben."

"We'll see to it that they don't. Stay there, we can show ourselves out. I'll be in touch later."

"Do you want my phone number or do you already have it?"

Sara turned to Carla who flicked through her notebook. "I only have your address."

Mrs Connor gave Carla the number, and she jotted it down.

She remained seated while they put their shoes back on and showed themselves out of the house. Sara caught a glimpse of Mr Connor loitering at the kitchen doorway, but neither of them spoke.

Sara closed the door behind her on the way out.

"That was tough," Carla said, stating the obvious.

"It's never easy. Quick, get in the car, it's just beginning to rain again."

"Any thoughts so far?"

Sara clicked her seatbelt into place and shrugged. "I'm on the fence about Tess. Maybe it's a case of a clash of person-alities."

"Yeah, I wondered that, too. Can you imagine anyone going out of their way to batter themselves like that? I can't."

"Yep, and you know how protective parents can be. He probably never did anything wrong in their eyes."

"I agree. But maybe we should keep an open mind on Tess all the same, for now."

CHAPTER 2

hen they arrived, the manager of the sports shop was tending to a complaint from an irate customer. Sara and Carla stood off to the side, pretending to be interested in some of the latest trainers available on the market until he joined them.

"Sorry for the delay, ladies. You wanted to see me?"

Sara and Carla flashed their warrant cards.

"Would it be possible to speak to you in your office, Mr Grant?" Sara asked.

"Yes. Are we in some kind of trouble, or is this a personal visit?"

"We'll let you know soon."

"Come this way."

They walked through the racks of branded trainers and sports shoes and he opened a door at the rear of the shop.

"Sophie," he said, "I shouldn't be too long. Give me a shout if you need me."

Sophie was dealing with a customer at the till and raised her thumb.

He laughed. "A girl of few words. We're a man down

today. I can't get hold of my assistant manager, Ben, which is unusual. He's never let me down before."

Sara smiled but didn't reply until they had passed through the small hallway and set foot in his office.

He scrabbled around, clearing chairs that had layers of shoeboxes on them, and then offered for them to take a seat. "Sorry, we have limited space around here. Nowhere to put the returned shoes so they get dumped in here. It's not ideal."

"Don't worry," Sara replied. She sat in the chair closest to the desk which was as cluttered as the chairs had been.

He sat down heavily and sighed. "One day there'll be enough hours in the day to tend to everything."

"I doubt it, I know that feeling myself. The joys of being in charge, eh?"

"Exactly. It can be somewhat tedious rather than a plea-sure, I'm sure you'll agree."

"Absolutely. Anyway, I'd better fill you in on why we're here today. It's about your assistant manager, Ben Connor."

His expression darkened. "Don't tell me he's been sitting in a police cell all night."

"If only that were true. Sadly, I have some bad news to share with you. This morning, Mr Connor's body was found in an alley."

"What are you saying? His body? Are you telling me that he's *dead*?"

"Yes. He's been murdered."

He flung himself back in his chair and immediately bounced forward again. "I'm struggling to comprehend what you're saying. Have you caught the person who did it? Do you know why? How do you know it was murder and that he wasn't killed in a freak accident or something like that?"

"All very plausible questions. I can't really go into detail about his death except to say that he was found tortured at the crime scene."

Mr Grant physically gagged. "Oh God, not Ben. He was such a good bloke. Never took life seriously, that one, well, not around here."

"Do you know much about his relationship?"

"With Tess, is that what you're asking?"

"Yes. Did he mention her much?"

"All the time. What are you getting at? You're not telling me you think she's guilty of killing him, are you?"

"No. I'm merely asking what their relationship was like. Did he speak about his home life much?"

Mr Grant's gaze dropped to his hands that were twisting nervously on the desk. He didn't reply so Sara asked the question again.

"Did he, Mr Grant?"

"I think so."

It was the way he said it that made Sara doubt if his reply was truthful. "You sound unsure. Is there something you're not telling us?"

He tutted and shook his head. "It's not really my place to tell you."

"Tell us what? Do I have to remind you that I'm leading a murder inquiry here, sir?"

"I'm sorry. I know that, of course I do. I find myself in an invidious position."

"In what respect?"

"I was sworn to secrecy, and now you're trying to force the information out of me." He seemed agitated and ran a hand through his short black hair and heaved out a sigh.

"I'm sorry. All we're trying to ascertain is the truth, Mr Grant. If you're guilty of holding back vital information, then you could find yourself in all sorts of trouble."

"Are you threatening me?"

"Call it a warning," Sara replied, her stomach clenching. "What do you know?"

He picked up a pen and twirled it through his fingers while he contemplated his answer.

Sara felt the need to prompt him one more time. "Do I have to remind you that your employee and colleague has lost his life?"

"I'm aware of that fact, thank you. That's where my dilemma lies."

Sara frowned and tilted her head to the side. "Why?"

He leant back against the headrest. "Jesus, this is so difficult for me. I know I should come out and tell you but I'm worried about the consequences."

"I still can't understand your hesitation, not when I've informed you that Ben Connor is dead. His home life situation might be the cause of his murder, and yet here you are, suppressing what could be vital information, why?"

He sucked in a breath and let it out slowly, then mumbled, "He was having an affair."

The words came as a sucker punch to Sara. She glanced wide-eyed at Carla who shook her head in disgust.

"Do you know with whom?" Sara demanded.

He pointed at the door. "Sophie, out there."

"Okay, this throws a whole different light on the investigation. I appreciate you being honest with us, eventually. How long has the affair been going on, do you know?"

"No. Look, you're going to have to speak to Sophie about the ins and outs of it. I found them snogging in the stockroom last week. I blew my top at them. The next day, I got in touch with head office, made them aware of the situation. They weren't happy and told me I had to sack one of them. I couldn't do that. It's in their contracts, so the firm has them by the short and curlies. The only other solution was for Ben to be shifted out. I was furious with them both, I admit for purely selfish reasons. They're both exceptional workers, and the shop was ticking over nicely because it had a great working environment, until I caught them at it. Why can't people just behave themselves, it's not much to ask, is it?"

"I agree. Did you manage to sit down with Ben and find out why he was having an affair?"

He shrugged and sat forward again. "You only have to look at Sophie to know the answer to that one. She's really pretty."

Sara nodded, admitting he was right. "Did he ever confide in you about what was going on at home?"

He frowned. "No. Should he have?"

Sara's mouth twisted as she debated whether to tell him about the abuse or not. In the end, she decided she had to, otherwise the dilemma would be hanging over her for the rest of the day. "When we showed up at his home earlier, to break the news to Tess, she had a black eye and was limping."

"That's a shame. Ben never mentioned she'd been in an accident. Did she say how it happened?"

"After a while she confided in us that Ben had beaten her up. Were you aware that he was an abuser?"

"Fuck! Seriously? I would never have believed that about him. Bloody hell, you've knocked the wind out of my sails with that one."

"I can tell. What about Sophie, is there a chance she knew?"

"How would I know? This is the first I'm hearing about it. I'm shocked and appalled by the revelation. I'm sure she would be as well, if she had found out the truth."

"Do you think we could have a word with Sophie?"

"I think that would be for the best. I'll take over from her out front and send her through."

"Keep it quiet as to why we're here, if you would."

"Of course." His lips parted in a brief smile, and he left the room.

"Well, that came as a blow to him," Sara said in a low voice.

"Didn't it just? A case of Ben wearing a different mask when he's at work, maybe?"

"Definitely. It's going to be interesting to see what Sophie has to say."

"Either way, I sense there are going to be tears." Carla groaned.

A faint knock on the door interrupted their conversation.

Sara turned in her seat and said, "Come in." The door opened, and she smiled to welcome Sophie into the room. "Hi, Sophie, thanks for speaking with us. Take a seat."

"Thanks." Sophie dashed around the desk and fell into the chair. "What's this about? The boss refused to tell me. The only thing he was willing to say was that it was serious. How? What did he mean?"

"Let me introduce myself. I'm DI Sara Ramsey, and this is my partner, DS Carla Jameson."

"Okay. I hate being in the dark. What's going on? Have I done something wrong? I've never been in trouble with the police before."

"No. Let me put your mind at ease there. It's nothing you've done. We're here to share some bad news about a colleague of yours, Ben Connor."

"Wh… what news?"

"Unfortunately, Ben has been found dead." Sara paused to let the information sink in.

Sophie shook her head and gasped. "I don't believe you."

"I'm sorry for your loss. I understand that you and Ben were more than just colleagues, is that true?"

Sophie sobbed and covered her eyes with her hand. "I can't believe it. He's gone! This can't be true." She wiped her running nose on the sleeve of her sweatshirt.

"I'm afraid it is true. I'm now leading a murder inquiry."

"No, he was killed? How? Who did it, do you know?"

"Our investigation is still in the initial stages at the moment. Clues and evidence are very thin on the ground, which is why we're here, to obtain answers. I know how difficult this must be for you but I'm going to need you to be as open and honest with us as you can be. Is that okay, Sophie?"

"Yes, of course. I've got nothing to hide. I'll do anything and everything I can to help you. I can't believe it. This is so hard to take in. He was…"

Sara inclined her head after Sophie broke off from what she was saying and glanced down at her hands. "What were you about to say?"

"A decent bloke, but then I stopped myself because of what was going on between us."

"The affair?"

"Yes, although I doubt if you could call it that."

"Care to enlighten us? How long had you been seeing each other?"

"We weren't, not really. The boss caught us kissing last week…"

"Was that the first time?"

"No. I suppose I've been flirting with him for months, and the kiss just happened out of the blue. Neither of us was expecting it. You know what it's like." Her cheeks tinged with colour.

"Were you aware that he was in a long-term relationship? That he was living with his girlfriend?"

She nodded and chewed her lip. "I know. I felt bad about that."

"So, what was going to happen next, had you discussed it?"

"No, not really. We were going to go out on a date and see how things worked out. I'm sorry, I know you must think badly of me, but sometimes it's really hard to control your feelings."

"I've never had that problem myself, but that's a different story. Are you single, Sophie?"

Her gaze drifted off to the left. "Yes, I dumped my boyfriend about a month ago."

"Can I ask why? Don't tell me, because you had feelings for Ben, is that right?"

"Yes and no. He was a dick. Always letting me down. Once Ben showed an interest in me, I decided there was more to life than being treated like a nobody."

"So, instead, you went after a man who was already involved with someone?"

"Please, you have to understand that I resisted the temptation for ages. Working with Ben, day in and day out... well, it wasn't easy. He was charismatic, had a good sense of humour and treated me right, compared to Wayne."

"We're going to need Wayne's surname and address."

"What? Why? No... you can't think he did this to Ben? No way, he wouldn't have it in him."

"How was he after you broke up with him?"

Sophie paused to consider the question. "He wasn't happy, but Christ, I don't think he's capable of going out there and killing someone."

"How well do you know him?"

"I'd been going out with him for over six months, and he never showed any signs of aggression or anger before I dumped him."

"Sometimes they're the type of people you need to keep a close eye on."

"No way. I don't believe it, he wouldn't dare."

Sara raised an eyebrow. "Are you confident about that?"

"No, I guess I'm not. God, what a bloody mess."

"We're going to need to have a chat with him all the same. His address and surname, if you would?"

"Wayne Hunt. He lives in a flat close to the river in town. Flat thirty-eight in the Crossland Estate. Do you know it?"

Sara glanced at Carla. Her partner nodded.

Sara turned back to Sophie. "Yes, we know it. Where does he work?"

"He's a bus driver. He doesn't get home until six-thirtyish. So there will be no point in you going over there before then."

"Thanks for the information. We'll take the risk and see where it leads us. Going back to Ben, what were his intentions, do you know?"

"His intentions? Regarding what?"

"Living with Tess. Was he going to dump her? Or carry on seeing both of you?"

"I wouldn't have stood for that. Like I said, we were going to go on a date, see if we were compatible, and then discuss things later."

Sara was riled up inside by the woman's words. *What about Tess? She didn't matter, obviously.* "Did Ben mention what his relationship with Tess was like?"

"He told me they were going through a rough patch. Don't all relationships?"

"Not to that extent, no," Sara bristled uncharacteristically.

"What extent? What are you talking about?"

"Ben abused Tess. If you went around there to see her, you'd see the proof for yourself."

Sophie gasped and slapped a hand over her gaping mouth.

"Sorry if that comes as a shock to you. I guess we don't really know what a person is capable of until we live with them, do we?"

Sophie's hand dropped onto the desk with a thud. "I'm

sorry. I don't want to believe this, not of Ben. He wasn't like that at all. He was kind, fun-loving, and people loved him. A popular sort of guy who you'd be happy to call a friend."

"Or go out with?"

"Yes."

"It's what goes on behind closed doors that matters, isn't it?"

She gulped and paused for a few long moments. "I can't believe it. Maybe she's behind him getting killed. What if she's pretending that Ben beat her up? I've heard there are women out there who do that kind of thing, I read it in a magazine not so long ago. This girl got fed up with her fella and started seeing another bloke, they came up with this plan to kill the boyfriend and beat her up at the same time but, after a while, the police saw through the lies and deceit."

"It's something we're aware of and will be investigating along with other evidence that comes our way."

"Glad to hear it. Women can be just as manipulative as men."

"That sounds like the voice of experience. Is it?"

"I've had my fair share of crappy relationships and friendships to know that sometimes people aren't always what they want the world to perceive them to be... if that makes sense?"

"It does. That's what we have to deal with on a daily basis. Since dumping Wayne, has he been in touch with you?"

"No. He accepted the relationship had come to a standstill, although he was angry at the time. Now you're causing doubts to enter my mind. He couldn't be behind this, could he?"

"Honest answer is, we can't and won't be ruling anything out. Ben was tortured before he was killed. That leads us to believe that someone had a possible grievance with him. It's up to us to uncover what that was."

"I'd be looking closer to home. You can't dismiss Tess."

"So you've already stated. Do you know her at all?"

"No. I've seen her in here once or twice, never really spoken to her as such."

"And yet you've been keen to point the finger in her direction."

Sophie sniffled and wiped her nose. "I'm sorry. Maybe I'm too upset to think straight. Please, don't think badly of me. I know I shouldn't have kissed Ben and flirted with him, but I swear, it didn't go any further than that."

"Thank you. One last question, if I may? Where were you last night between the hours of nine p.m. and seven this morning?"

"Why? Oh God, I can't believe you're asking me this. I was at home."

"Can someone corroborate your alibi?"

"No. Shit! You can't think that I had anything to do with Ben's murder. I wouldn't. I couldn't. You have to believe me." Her voice rose in a frantic crescendo.

"Calm down, Sophie. It was a simple question. Maybe you won't be as quick to point the finger at someone else in the future."

"You mean Tess?"

"Yes, you were pretty adamant about her involvement but neglected to think about the consequences of voicing such concerns."

"I… I didn't mean anything by it. You asked my opinion, and I gave it. If I did something wrong, then I'm sorry. It wasn't my intention to muddy the waters of your inquiry."

"Ah, but nevertheless, that's exactly what you did."

She sighed. "I apologise. Can I take back my accusation?"

"No, it's too late for that. We'll cover all angles during our investigation, there's no doubt about that. Is there anything else you can tell us about Ben? You were friends, right?

55

Before you kissed him, did he confide in you? Tell you if he was in any kind of trouble?"

"He never mentioned anything. We weren't that close. Not close enough that he would confide in me."

"Did you ever see anyone lingering near the shop? Waiting for his shift to end, perhaps?"

She paused to think and pulled the sleeve over her hand. "No, I don't think so. I'm sorry, my head is spinning right now. Can you leave me a card and I'll get back to you later if anything comes to mind?"

"I was about to suggest the same. How many staff work here?"

"The three of us plus a couple of Saturday kids. Both boys are around seventeen to eighteen."

"Thanks. Here's my card." Sara slid it across the desk.

Sophie picked it up and stared at it. "How do you do it? The job? When you have to grill people who have lost someone they care about?"

Sara shrugged. "It takes all sorts to make a world. My team is special, we care about what matters in our community. We go the extra mile it takes to bring people to justice. If that means that we step on a few toes along the way, then so be it."

"How do you detach yourself from the horrors you see? You said that Ben had been tortured. I don't want to know the ins and outs of what happened to him, I'd never have a decent night's sleep again."

"We just do. If we didn't then people would get away with the crimes they have committed and probably go on to commit even worse ones in the future. We rely on people such as yourself to be open and honest when we speak to them. We can generally see through people's lies, and when that happens, it leads us to think those people have something to hide."

"I see. I'd better get back to work now," Sophie added swiftly. "I hope you find the answers and the mystery of Ben's death is solved soon. Will you let us know?"

"We can't promise to consult everyone we speak with. You'll find out by listening to the news or reading the local paper."

"Ah, I'm not bothered about the news. Maybe that's a generation fault."

"Probably. Thanks for speaking with us. We'll come back to the shop with you."

The three of them left the manager's office to find Mr Grant standing by the door, one eye on the shop and the other on the hallway to his office.

"Everything all right?" he directed his question to Sophie.

"Yes, I think so. I might be a bit quiet the rest of the day."

He placed a hand on her shoulder and squeezed it. "If you need some time out just tell me. I can't let you go home, though, what with being short-staffed."

Sophie nodded. "I know. I'll be fine. The officers and I have had a good chat. I think things are a lot clearer in my mind now."

He seemed puzzled by her statement. "You get back to work, and I'll be with you shortly. We've got the order to put in later. I need to get on with that when I'm done here."

With an awkward smile, Sophie scurried back behind the counter.

"How did she get on?" Mr Grant asked.

"She was fine. She answered all our questions which is the main thing. Sophie is really upset about Ben, so maybe go easy on her today."

"She'll be fine. I'll start cracking a few of my jokes, that usually brings a smile to her face."

Sara smiled. "If you insist. Just be aware that she's

received some shocking news that might be hard for her to process once it sinks in."

"Haven't we all? I've already been on the phone to head office. They're sorting out a replacement for Ben as we speak."

"I see. That was quick."

"You can't take your foot off the pedal in business, not in this business anyway."

"I suppose. Thanks for chatting with us, Mr Grant. I'll leave you one of my cards. If you think of anything we should know, please do get in touch."

"I will. I doubt it, but yes, you have my word I'll get on the blower right away."

Sara and Carla left the shop and went back to the car they had parked in the Waitrose car park close to the precinct.

"Looks like we've got a few suspects on our radar already," Carla said.

Sara pressed the key fob, and the doors clunked open. "It seems that way. Let's get back to the station. I'll make a note to drop by and have a word with Wayne Hunt on the way home this evening."

"Makes sense, unless you ring the bus company, see if he has a lunch hour at the canteen. We could catch him there."

"You ring them en route then." Sara started the car and drove through the town centre.

As suspected, Carla failed to pin the bus company down. Wayne Hunt would be available at the end of his shift and not before, as they were also short-staffed.

It appears to be the way of the world since Covid hit us.

SARA GATHERED the team together and went over the details they had obtained about the crime scene, plus the relatives, and last of all, what the workmates had told them during the course of the morning.

After hearing the extent of the victim's injuries, Barry sucked in a breath and winced. "Sounds like someone was out for revenge. My money is on the girlfriend. Maybe she's paid someone to teach him a lesson and it got out of hand."

Sara waved her hand from side to side. "Carla and I discussed this in the car, we're in two minds about it. Yes, we're going to look into it further, but I don't want everyone's efforts to be focussed on the girlfriend. Christine, can you do the usual on the bank accounts for me? I want Ben's and Tess's checked over."

"I'll get on it right away, boss."

"I want the usual carried out regarding the CCTV, nearest cameras to the alley. Not sure there's going to be much available in that part of the city but, nevertheless, let's see what we can gather. I'll leave that in your capable hands, Craig."

He nodded and tapped on his keyboard.

"The only loose end we have at present is talking to the ex-boyfriend of the girl the victim was having an affair with," Sara said. "I'll be doing that on the way home, but we can definitely dig into his background in the meantime. See if he has any kind of record that may be of interest to the investigation. Apart from that, we're going to be reliant on what the pathologist and SOCO have for us. I'll be in my office, should anything come to light in the meantime."

Sara left the team to get on with their tasks and drifted into her office with her coffee in her hand. Before tackling her dreaded admin duties, she rang Mark. "Sorry to disturb you at work. Can you talk?"

"Briefly. I'm in between dealing with two aggressive pussies who have left their mark on me in the past. I barely scraped by without a scratch from the last one."

"Ouch, sounds painful. I wanted to make you aware that I'll be a little late home tonight."

"Oh, nothing wrong with your dad, is there?"

"Damn, that reminds me, I need to check up on him during the day as well. No, I digress, we were called to a bad murder scene this morning. That came out wrong, not that there are ever any *good* murder scenes."

He chuckled. "I knew what you meant, and?"

"And, I need to speak to a person of interest but I can only get hold of him this evening, not during the day as he's a bus driver. Believe me, I've tried."

"That's a shame. You work hard enough during the day as it is without giving up part of your evening as well."

"I know. Thankfully it doesn't happen that often. Want me to pick up a takeaway on the way home as compensation?"

"No, I'll throw something together. What time shall I expect you?"

"Latest seven, maybe seven-fifteen."

He laughed. "I'll do dinner for seven-thirty, just in case then. I have to fly now. Love you."

"I love you, too, not just because you're a talented vet but also because you're the most understanding husband a woman could ever wish to have."

"What a wonderful compliment, if only you meant it."

Sara gasped. "I do, you cheeky sod. See you later. Watch out for the angry pussies on your horizon." She hung up quickly before he could give a witty retort. She sighed and got stuck into the onerous chore she despised the most and hoped that someone would come to her rescue soon.

It took a while for Carla to do just that. "Thought you should know that the bank accounts came back clear for Tess and Ben. A few debts on both accounts, no huge payments out, only the regular type of thing: Amazon, takeaway outlets and the usual utility direct debits on both."

"Okay. Have you found anything on Wayne Hunt?"

"Interestingly enough, yes. He has an ABH against him from seven years ago. He was arrested after whacking a bloke inside a nightclub. The bouncers tried to restrain him and remove him from the premises, but he lashed out and broke the nose of one of them."

"So they hit him with a charge."

"That's right. Big burly men like that, squabbling like infants, I bet that was fun to watch."

Sara frowned. "Only if you have a twisted mind." She glanced at her watch, aware that time was marching on. Her tummy rumbled. "We missed out on lunch today."

"I hadn't noticed what the time was. Want me to see if there's anything left at the baker's?"

"I'm not sure if I fancy anything heavy. Maybe a piece of fruit will do." She rummaged in the drawer next to her, hoping to find an apple. There wasn't one. "I thought I put an apple in here last week, I must have eaten it without realising."

"Eww... you keep fruit in your drawers?"

"Yes, for emergencies. Get that disgusted look off your face, you're far from perfect, I saw what was lurking in your drawer as I passed your desk the other day. You need to throw away all those chocolate wrappers."

Carla pulled another face at her. "Yes, boss. What can I get for you?"

"I fancy a banana. Do you want some money?"

Carla winked. "I'm sure I can stretch to one of those. Hey, I got off lightly, forking out for a cheap lunch. Makes a change."

Sara grimaced. "If you say so." She got back to answering

61

her emails until Carla reappeared with a banana and a mug of coffee.

"Here you go, delivery service with a smile."

"You're an angel. Thanks, Carla. No news on the CCTV, I take it?"

Carla sat in the chair opposite and said, "Nothing yet, but Craig has extended the search." Then she took a chunk out of her large red apple.

"I think that's going to be a waste of time. I'm debating whether I should call a press conference or not."

"Why the hesitation?"

Sara put her half-eaten banana, skin down, on a tissue, and lifted her mug to her lips. "I'm not sure. What can I tell them? Apart from that the victim was tortured and then killed down an alley?"

Carla frowned. "That doesn't usually prevent you from holding one. What's the problem this time?"

"I'm not sure there is one. There's something in my gut holding me back."

"Want me to see if the house-to-house enquiries have come back with anything?"

"You can do that, although if anything had come up, I'm sure Jeff would have got in touch with me."

Carla rose from her seat and took her apple and drink with her. "I'll check now."

"Thanks."

Carla poked her head around the door a few moments later. "Jeff said some of the neighbours reported hearing a scream at around ten forty-five, but they put it down to someone messing around while they were drunk. Apart from that, nothing worth mentioning."

"Great. I know that alley isn't used much at night, but even so, I give up with people being aware of their surroundings these days. If it doesn't concern them directly then they couldn't give a rat's arse what's happening around them."

"Have you finished?"

Sara raised an eyebrow. "Too much?"

Carla nodded. "I've heard it all before."

"Get you. I apologise for repeating myself."

"It's fine, just don't make a habit of it. Do you need anything else, apart from me getting out of your hair?"

"No, thanks. Let the team get off at five. Are you going to visit Hunt with me?"

"Do you want me to?"

"I wouldn't mind, but if you've got something else planned for this evening, I can go alone. It makes no odds to me either way."

"I haven't, and you're not going alone to see a man with an ABH offence sitting on his record, got that?"

"Thanks, Carla. We'll head over there about sixish and hope he's not the type to stop off at the pub on his way home."

"I'm sure it'll only be local if he does."

"We'll see."

Carla left her to it, and Sara decided to check in on her father while she had a few minutes spare. "Dad, it's me. How are you today?"

"How wonderful to hear from you, sweetheart. I'm fine, getting the mobile home ready to set off for a week's holiday."

"Oh, that's news to me. Are you going alone this time or is Lesley going with you?"

"I thought I'd venture off alone. I have to do it sometime, why not now while the weather is still fairly warm? Even if we have been subjected to more rain than they've forecast the past week."

"Why not indeed. I envy you. It's been months since Mark and I have spent any decent time off together."

"You only have to ask, you know you can borrow the van anytime you like, providing I haven't made any arrangements to go away. The break will do you some good. You both work far too hard, in my opinion."

"It's called life, Dad. We'd love to take you up on your offer next year, maybe in the spring."

"You only have to shout."

"Anyway, where are you heading this time?"

"Thought I'd take a quick sprint down to Somerset. Your mother and I used to love it down there."

"Are you going to visit anywhere in particular?"

Her father sighed a little. "We used to enjoy visiting Wookey Hole, you know, the Mendip Hills area."

"That would be lovely, Dad. I'm sure you'll have a smashing time. Just don't get caught out by the weather. Isn't Somerset prone to flooding now and again?"

"Let's face it, love, where isn't these days?"

"Fair point. Will we see you before you go?"

"I'm leaving on Sunday afternoon. Can you squeeze me in for dinner before I set off?"

"Come to dinner on Sunday, how's that? It'll save you having to stop off to get something to eat."

"Sounds perfect. Can I put in a request for dinner?"

Sara laughed, having an inkling what he was about to ask next. "If you must."

"I'd like a nice piece of roast pork, is that possible?"

"I'll see if Mark won't mind rustling one up for you. He's the expert with that dish."

"Only if it's no bother for yourselves."

Sara picked up a pen and fed it through her fingers. "I'm sure it won't be. See you at around twelve on Sunday."

"Looking forward to it already. Thanks for checking up on me, love."

"Not checking up, checking in to ensure you're doing well, Dad. Just shout if you need anything."

"I will."

She ended the call with a smile, and her mother's image entered her mind. She thought how proud her mother would be if she could see how well her father was coping since he'd lost her. In truth, her father had surprised all of them in the months since their mother's passing. It had been touch and go to begin with, but they had overcome several issues that her father was determined to get past. It had been his idea to sell up, buy a flat in town and get himself a mobile home so he could travel the country in his retirement, rather than sit at home dwelling on the fact he was old and alone now.

He was to be admired. It took guts to do what he had while he was still grieving. He'd turned his life around in the six months since her mother had died. She couldn't be prouder of him.

Back to work, admin was calling. She stretched the knots out of her back and went into battle again for another couple of hours. Sara called Lorraine regarding the funeral and got back to Ben's mother with the answer as promised.

THEY CHOSE to take two cars to the location and parked close to the block of flats where Wayne Hunt resided. Sara had her warrant card in her hand, ready to shove it in his face the second he opened the door to them. There was a slight delay but, eventually, the front door opened to reveal a man with red hair and matching beard. His blue eyes creased up as soon as he laid eyes on them.

"Can I help you?"

Sara and Carla both showed their IDs, and his shoulders slouched.

"Mr Hunt, is it possible for us to have a quick chat with you?" Sara asked.

Just then, a teenager rode past them on a bike.

"I've warned you before, Taylor, get away from my flat or your father's going to feel my fist in his face."

Sara turned. The youth gave Hunt the finger and cycled off.

"Is there a problem here?" she asked.

"Nope. It's been dealt with. You were saying you wanted a chat with me, about what?"

"It would be better if we spoke inside, unless you want your nosey neighbours to overhear. It's up to you."

"Jesus, I've only been in a couple of minutes. Were you sitting outside, waiting for me to show up?"

"No, we were aware of what time your shift finished and took a gamble that you would come straight home."

"Okay. What's this about?"

He reluctantly let them in, and they carried on the conversation in the snug hallway. He immediately became defensive, crossed his arms and leant against the wall. It was clear to Sara that he had no intention of offering to let them anywhere near the rest of the flat.

"I'm the Senior Investigating Officer on a murder inquiry."

He pushed off the wall and stood upright, his arms still folded. "Who's dead? One of my mates?"

"A Mr Ben Connor. Do you know him?"

His eyes narrowed once more, and his chest inflated and deflated a few times. "I know him."

"How well do you know him?"

"Well enough to know he was shagging my girlfriend."

"Your girlfriend?" Sara asked innocently. "Who might that be?"

"What is this? You know all this shit, otherwise you wouldn't be here in the first place. I know what games you get up to, trying to trip folks up."

Carla took out her notebook and flicked to a clean page.

"Your girlfriend's name?"

"Sophie," he relented eventually. "What about her? Is she the one who dropped my name into the mix?"

"I can't reveal my sources, Mr Hunt," Sara said. "What I need to know is where you were between nine last night and seven this morning."

He grinned and toppled against the wall again. "I was at a concert with a couple of friends. I suppose you'll be wanting their numbers next, won't you?"

"That would be great, thank you."

He unfolded his arms, withdrew his phone from his back pocket and scrolled through his contacts. "This is Seb's." He flashed the phone at Carla to write down the information. And then he searched for another number. "And Jack's. They'll both vouch for me."

"What concert did you attend?"

"I doubt if you'd know them, it's a heavy metal band. Local, they are."

"The name of the band?"

"Rocks Off."

"Nice name," Sara said. "And where was the concert held?"

"At a pub. They have a conference room out the back, it's soundproofed, so we didn't have to watch the noise we were making. Which was a bonus, the crowd had a blast, and spirits were high."

"We'll check your alibi out, thank you. Have you been in touch with Sophie since she called off the relationship?"

"You know the answer to that one. No, I haven't, which is what she would have told you, I hope."

"She did. How did you feel about the breakup?"

"At the time I was pissed off but then I got used to being on my own again and liked it. I don't miss the cheating bitch, if that's going to be your next question."

"It wasn't. I get the impression you're still angry about the situation."

"Nah. Not in the slightest. She was a bit of a leech, always hanging around when I needed my freedom, you know what it's like during the season when the football is on and your girl can't stand it. I've been brought up worshipping my team, and no girl is going to change that, either now or in the future."

"You seem a very determined and strong-willed character, Mr Hunt."

"Meaning what?" he challenged, throwing back his slouching shoulders.

"It's merely an observation. Have you seen Ben lately?"

"Nope. Why would I?"

"Not around town? Or at the pub?"

"I said no. What are you saying? That my fingerprints were on the murder weapon or something?"

"Oh no, nothing like that. I'm just trying to ascertain when or if you saw the victim lately."

"And my answer was no. I don't know him as such. I only know—sorry, knew—him as being my girlfriend's boss, or one of them, and him taking advantage of her."

"Is that what she told you?"

"Not in so many words. I'm wise enough to figure out the pair of them had been shagging behind my back for weeks."

"We were led to believe that they hadn't slept together and the relationship had only just begun."

"Bollocks. Someone has been lying to you. What you've got to work out is, why?"

Maybe he has a point. Could Sophie be behind Ben's murder? Thinking about her reaction to his death, she didn't seem that upset, not really. Not in my opinion.

"Are you aware of where Ben lived?"

"What sort of question is that?"

"One I need an answer to. Did you know in what part of town Ben lived?"

"I think somewhere down by the river, not sure of the exact address."

"What about his personal life?"

"What is this? I couldn't give a shit about the bastard. All I knew was that he'd been screwing around with Sophie. There's no coming back from that, not for her."

"Did you know he was living with someone?"

He shook his head and shrugged. "It doesn't surprise me. He seemed the type who wanted the best of both worlds. Looks like someone put paid to him dipping his wick here, there and everywhere, doesn't it?"

"So it would seem. Did Sophie ever mention him before they started having an affair behind your back?"

"Yep, she was always going on about him, saying how smart he was."

"And that ticked you off?" Sara asked.

"Yes and no. I think she was having a dig at me for being a bus driver. That never sat well with her. The thing is, I enjoy what I do. All right, the roads around Hereford can be a nightmare to deal with most days, but the money is okay for the hours you put in, and I get weekends off."

"Did Sophie ever talk about Ben's girlfriend, Tess?"

He frowned and shook his head. "Not that I can remember, why? Are you thinking she's behind this fella's murder now, instead of me?"

"I never said you were behind it. The purpose of our visit is to seek out the facts. As I'm sure you'll appreciate, if someone is unfaithful to their partner and the other party shows up dead one day, the police are bound to be suspicious of all the people involved."

He hitched up a shoulder. "And the girlfriend, you need to keep her in the frame, too. There are two wronged people here, not just me."

"We are, don't worry. That's all we need for now. We'll check out your alibi with your two friends."

"You do that. I've got nothing to hide. And for the record, I'm *not* sorry he's dead. There, I've said it."

Sara smiled. "I can understand your anger."

"I doubt it. But I don't give a shit either way."

"Thanks for taking the time to speak with us, Mr Hunt. Enjoy the rest of your evening."

"Yeah, I intend to."

He opened the front door and slammed it shut after Sara and Carla had left the flat.

"Nice chap," Carla mumbled.

"Aggrieved and rightly so. But yes, full of anger as well. I'm not ready to dismiss him as a suspect yet, not quite. Time to call it a day. Thanks for coming with me, Carla. You can start a bit later in the morning, if you want."

"Rubbish. Less than half an hour extension to my working day, it's fine. You worry too much."

"Yeah, I've been told that several times in the past."

Carla stopped and faced her. "Everything all right, Sara? Only you seem down in the mouth about something all of a sudden."

Sara dismissed her partner's concern with a wave of the hand. "I'm fine. It's been a long day. I think it's catching up on me now."

They reached their cars, and Carla accepted her excuse

for what it was, the truth. "Right. I'll see you bright and early then. Let it go tonight and enjoy what's left of your evening with Mark."

"I will. And you have a good one as well. Don't forget what we discussed earlier."

"Already in hand. I'm building up to having a frank and open discussion about what both of us want. Fingers crossed Des is okay with me having a mind of my own and listening to the doubts that are weaving their way through my mind."

Sara tapped the side of her nose. "Trust me, he'll be fine. He's not like other men, give him some credit for that, love."

Carla opened her car door. "Yeah, okay. I'll let you know how it goes in the morning."

"Drive carefully." Sara dropped behind her steering wheel and rang Mark. "I'm on my way home now. Do we need anything from the shop?"

"No. It's all in hand. I picked up some odds and ends on the way back myself. See you soon."

"Twenty minutes at the most." She ended the call.

Sara drove away from the block of flats which was right next door to the flats where her brother, Tim, was found dead. She tried to shrug off the feeling of remorse that always charged through her when she thought about him. Before his death, he had become more and more reliant on drugs to see him through the day which, in the end, had meant she had turned her back on him when he had needed her the most. Sometimes she lay awake at night, wondering if Tim had been reunited with their mother and if he had returned to his old self again. The cheeky chappie, without a care in the world weighing heavily on his shoulders, the man he used to be during their youth.

Families, you can't live with them and you can't live without them!

71

CHAPTER 3

Owen searched through his holdall for the appropriate gear to wear. This time he would be in full disguise. He handled the woollen balaclava and tucked it into the pocket of his combat jacket until it would be required. Then he left his crummy surroundings to begin his adventure.

Under the cover of darkness, he travelled across the city on foot until the time was right for him to steal a vehicle. He'd had his eye on a certain make for a while now and had noticed one had showed up on a nearby estate, which he passed through several times a week. He'd take the plunge and steal it. Aware that it would be alarmed, he had the tools in his bag to combat any issues that might entail. His contact had told him what to do to access the vehicle and how to disable an alarm swiftly. Sure, the information had cost him money, but the guy appeared to know his way around cars from what he could tell, so Owen was willing to give it a go. His mate had also supplied him with fake numberplates to switch over, to keep the coppers at arm's length, for now.

He checked around him a final time and then swiftly worked his magic and jumped into the car. Laughing, he roared away from the busy road. The owner probably thought someone had knocked it to set off the alarm and ended up helping him out by turning it off with his key fob from inside the house. *Idiot, that'll teach you to be more alert next time.*

The engine purred the way he thought it would, like a dream. The pleasure was all his as he drove to the location. Again, he had watched and noted his second victim's routine for a few weeks. If only people realised what creatures of habit they could become. Still, he had it covered. Although the victim knew him, there was no doubt in his mind that he had the upper hand, showing up in the stolen vehicle. He would ensure this played out to his advantage or he'd go down fighting. The alternative wasn't in his remit. His determination to see the job through to its satisfactory conclusion was what continued to drive him on.

He drew up away from the streetlights and killed the engine. Hiding in the shadow of a large office building, next to the pub, he switched the numberplates and then settled back into his seat. He had arrived earlier than he'd anticipated and dipped his cap over his eyes to have a quick snooze. However, a nearby fracas between a couple of drunks disturbed his bout of relaxation. He grinned, watching the tanked-up louts take swings at each other in the hope they'd hit their target and knock seven bells out of their opponent. Both missed and fell flat on their faces. Undeterred, they got to their feet and took up their combative stances once more. A small crowd left the pub and cheered and goaded them. But exhaustion struck, and the two men ended up on the ground in fits of giggles.

Bloody idiots. If I didn't have plans for tonight, I'd stick around and give them a few tips in unarmed combat. It had been a speciality of mine, back in the day.

The two men grappled each other's arms and attempted to get to their feet but failed and collapsed several times when the laughter overwhelmed them again.

Shit! Here he is. He sat upright, recognising the build and gait of the man who had been his best friend for years. Through narrowed eyes, he watched Ned Frost help the two men to their feet before he turned right and began his trip home for the evening. Owen was aware Ned's home was a few streets away. Once they were a fair distance from the pub, he'd make his move. Up ahead, several people parked their cars, coming back from either a night out or a late shift from work. *Get past these morons and I can pounce on him.*

The Range Rover crawled along behind Ned. He appeared to be unaware of Owen's presence which gave him the confidence he was crying out for, in order to pull off his plan. Once the people had parked their cars and entered their homes, the road was deserted. His pulse quickened to the extent that a constant tap-tap-tap pounded in his neck and at the top of his leg. *I've got this. He deserves what's coming to him.* That's all he had to remember, that his former friend deserved what was about to take place.

He drove past Ned and pulled up a few feet ahead of him. Tugging the balaclava in place, he exited the vehicle, aware he was in the glare of the streetlights, not that it mattered. He was going through with this, he had no intention of turning back now.

Ned stared at Owen and frowned. "Something wrong with your face, mate? It looks kind of weird."

"Get in the car," Owen said, disguising his voice.

"What? Fuck off. I ain't going nowhere with you."

Owen took a couple of strides and clenched his fist. The

punch connected with Ned's jaw, sending him reeling into the hedge of the garden beside him.

"What the fuck? Who are you?"

"I told you, get in the car."

Ned staggered upright and then bolted as fast as his wayward legs would carry him, which turned out to be not that far. Within a few feet, Owen was on him. He tackled him to the ground and punched him a couple of times until Ned passed out. Blood poured from his broken nose and the slit in his cheek. Owen got to his feet and yanked Ned up and over his shoulder with ease. He opened the boot of the Rover and dumped Ned inside. *He'll be out for the count.*

He drove back to where he was staying, parked the Rover in the next road and hauled Ned out of the vehicle and over his shoulder again.

The dilapidated house was a welcome reprieve when he closed the door behind him and secured it with the heavy bolt he'd added the day he'd moved in. This place was temporary, it had been deemed unsafe and had a *To Be Condemned* notice pinned to the front door. But it would do for now. He had basic supplies to hand, a small camping stove, no electricity, and the room was lit by large church candles that he'd picked up from Poundland. Luckily, the water was still connected—someone had screwed up there. This place would do, for now, for what he had planned.

Ned stirred on the floor. Owen took the rope from his holdall and lashed it around Ned's wrists a few times, then secured it.

"What the...? What's going on? Shit... why does my nose hurt? What did you do to me?"

"Busted your nose into tiny pieces. You should have done what you were told, man."

Ned stared at him. Confusion surfaced in his former

friend's eyes. "Do I know you? Why are you doing this to me?"

Owen was surprised by how much Ned had sobered up since his capture. Initially, when he'd pulled up alongside him, Ned had staggered and was a touch unsteady on his feet. He let out an evil laugh. "Let's see, oh yes, because I can."

"But why? Answer me, damn you. I need to know what your intentions are."

Owen frowned. "Why do you *need* to know?"

Silence.

Owen dipped into his holdall and removed several items that he supposed some people would regard as torture implements. Ned gasped and sucked in a breath. Owen tore off a large strip of gaffer tape, anticipating Ned's scream or cry for help. He slapped the sticky tape over his mouth.

Ned's eyes widened, and his gaze drifted between Owen and the tools lying on the floor beside him. Owen picked up a set of pliers and tapped the metal tips on his palm. "Now then, where should I begin? Ah, yes, with this." He whipped off the balaclava and flattened his hair.

Ned's expression was one of horror and dread.

"Not who you expected, eh, mate?"

Ned said something behind the tape that sounded like, "Owen? What the fuck, man? I haven't laid eyes on you in years. What's going on? Why this?"

Owen grinned and took a step closer with the pliers. "The power one feels when they have a weapon of torture in their hands. It goes back to the days I was fighting the effing Taliban fuckers out in Afghanistan. I took pleasure in torturing the miserable shits, we all did. We took it in turn to dish out punishment many men have dreamt about giving to their enemies but have never been fortunate to be in the position to do it. We made them suffer. Most of them squirming and squealing like pigs with knives to their throats. Of course, you'd get the odd one who had balls of steel, or pretended to have, but we soon knocked that shit out of them. An enemy like no other, they were. I hated the bastards, each and every one of the sick, twisted fuckers. Ah, and there you are thinking who am I to call them such insulting names when I have you sitting here, trussed up. I'm right, aren't I?"

Ned slowly nodded.

"Well, I'm not going to sit back and disappoint you. I have work to do, so you'll forgive me if I don't stick around to chat with you." He grabbed Ned's arms and drew them towards him, but Ned fought back. He tugged so hard that they both toppled to the floor. Owen righted himself and punched Ned in the stomach. "You're going to wish you hadn't done that, *pal.*"

He yanked Ned's arm and sat him upright. With the pliers in hand, Owen grasped Ned's right forearm and pinched the pliers around his little finger. The crunching of bone shattered the silence in the room. Ned stared at him, the skin around his eyes screwed up in pain, and tears brimmed. He tried to cry out, but the tape held firm, deadening any sound. Ned shook his head and mumbled something else when Owen prepared yet another finger for the taking. Ned did his best to pull his hand away but was unsuccessful, and the further sound of crunching bones made them both stare at each other.

The pliers opened a third time, and Ned wrenched his hand from Owen's grasp only for him to grab the two broken fingers and squeeze tightly. Tears bulged and poured onto Ned's cheeks. He looked a broken man, but Owen was far from finished.

"Do you ever think about what you did to me?" he asked.

Tears sliding down his cheeks, Ned shook his head.

"Ah, wrong answer. I guess it hasn't quite sunk in yet, you know, what I'm capable of. Let's see if this will change your mind." Discarding Ned's damaged hand, Owen prepared the other hand. The pliers moved into position and, gripping the base of his little finger, he gave the pliers a quick twist, and the finger hung at an odd angle.

"Please, please?" Ned's muffled cry for help was distinctive enough to make out.

"What? Are you begging me for more? Of course, always willing to oblige, chum. This one might hurt, so prepare yourself."

Ned squeezed his eyes shut in an attempt to block out not only the image but the impending pain, or so Owen assumed.

"Eeny, meeny... which one shall I punish next?"

Ned played tug of war with his hand, but his injuries had weakened his resilience.

"You let me down. Abandoned me when I was at my lowest ebb. You can't expect me not to come down heavily on you. You deserve this. True friends never turn their backs on their friends, ever."

Ned's gaze met his, and Owen thought he saw a glint of an apology in their depths, but it was far too late for that. Actions meant more than words in his opinion, that's why he was pushing ahead with the torture. With each bone he broke in his former friend's fingers it healed a tiny part of him inside, or did it?

"My family was your family at one time. I came back home, needed a shoulder to cry on, an ear to listen to my woes, and you fucked off, didn't want to know me. A mate doesn't treat another bloke like that. You had no right turning your back on me. All I needed was for you to throw a comforting arm around my shoulders and buy me a pint, but you couldn't even do that, could you? Why? What went wrong?" He was tempted to rip the tape off but was fully aware of what would happen if he did. He dipped his head closer as Ned attempted to speak. "What's that? I can't hear you."

Ned mumbled what sounded like an apology, not once but numerous times, but it fell on deaf ears. Rage built inside Owen. This guy had been his best friend throughout school and had dumped him when he was counting on that friendship to pull him back from the abyss. He'd found himself on the verge of ending his life and needed to be surrounded by people he trusted. Ned had been the first to let him down. Someone he'd always relied on to be there for him, to get him out of jams when money was tight. What had happened to that friendship after all these years? His neck burned as the rage seared through his veins. Crushing a few of Ned's fingers was never going to be enough, he realised that now. He dipped into his holdall and extracted one of the saws. Not a hacksaw, he had decided a more substantial tool was needed this time for what he intended.

Ned's eyes almost dropped onto his pale cheeks. He shook his head as yet more tears surfaced and he tried to make himself heard.

Owen couldn't give a shit. One image was fixed in his head, and he was struggling to shift it. He wanted his friend to suffer, to die a gruesome death for giving up on him. Friends didn't do that to each other, *ever*. He angled the saw at the top of Ned's leg. Ned kicked out, squirmed, his resistance smothered by his restraints and the tape. *If he doesn't sit still then this is going to be harder than I thought.*

There was only one thing Owen could do to prevent Ned from moving, to knock him out, but where would the fun be in that? He wanted him conscious to witness what was going on. He glanced over his shoulder and spotted the chair. He rose and dragged Ned to his feet. Ned twisted and wriggled, but Owen held firm until they reached the chair, then he forced Ned to sit.

Another suppressed cry for help developed but was ignored by Owen. He returned to his holdall, removed another piece of rope and quickly tied Ned's legs to the chair.

"Right, now you're tethered, the really fun part can begin."

CHAPTER 4

wo days later

SARA WAS in a meeting with DCI Carol Price, going over a few new policies that needed clarifying by both of them, when the call came in. Carla thought she should bring it to Sara's attention immediately and sought her out in the DCI's office. Mary, DCI Price's secretary, knocked on the door and apologised for interrupting them.

"Sorry, ma'am. DS Jameson would like a word on an urgent matter, if possible."

Sara glanced over her shoulder.

DCI Price nodded and motioned for Carla to join them. "Come in. Is everything all right?"

"Sorry, I didn't mean to interrupt your meeting, but I thought you should know right away."

"Take a seat," Price instructed.

"What's going on, Carla?" Sara asked, puzzled by her partner's demeanour.

"Lorraine has called, requesting that we join her at a crime scene."

"Another torture-murder crime scene?" Sara asked, her stomach somersaulting several times.

Carla sighed and said, "Yes. Not a pleasant one either."

Sara glanced at DCI Price. "All right if I go, boss?"

Price flicked her hands. "Shoo, on your way. Keep me posted later about what's going on. This can be dealt with when we're both less busy. Good luck."

Sara and Carla tore out of the office and down the concrete stairs to the car park, neither of them saying anything until they jumped in the car and joined the flow of traffic on the main road.

"What else can you tell me?" Sara asked.

"Lorraine reckons that similar implements were used to mutilate the body."

Sara gulped. "Shit, your choice of words doesn't bode well."

"Except they're not mine, they're Lorraine's, and yes, I thought the same, which is why I felt the need to come and collect you. I don't usually interrupt your meetings with the chief."

"I know. How far is it?"

Up until now, Carla had been pointing out the route they needed to take. "Another five minutes, take a right at the end and then another left at the top and we should be at the location."

"I'm glad about one thing."

"What's that?"

"That we hadn't got around to having lunch yet."

Carla snorted. "You read my mind."

Lorraine's van was the first thing that caught Sara's attention as she turned into the street. She pulled up behind it, and they togged up in their protective suits, signed the Crime

Scene Log at the door of the property and entered the run-down building.

"You took your time," Lorraine chastised.

"It's lovely to see you, too. Yes, I'm well, thanks. You?"

"Bugger off. I'm not in the mood."

Sara took one look at the victim and immediately understood Lorraine's crabby mood. "Sorry. I'll stop messing around. What have we got?"

"I'm going out on a limb to tell you that I believe we're looking at a second victim."

"Any particular reason?"

"Everything about this crime is screaming the same as the first one, right down to the killer ensuring we know who the victim is." Lorraine held up a plastic Ziplock evidence bag with a wallet in it.

"Damn. Why is he doing this? I'm presuming the killer is a he, just because of the ferociousness of the attacks. Why dismember them?"

"From the experience I've gathered over the years, a killer dismembers as a final farewell to those he knew."

"A final farewell?"

"Killers usually dismember to disguise the crime, but that's not what we're seeing with this killer. Dismemberment is often an act of revenge. A way of expressing a certain degree of anger felt for the victim. There's the torture angle to consider as well, hence me saying it's the final farewell."

Sara shook her head. "Anger-filled murders are the worst to deal with in my opinion. Any clues as to who the killer is? Footprints perhaps?"

Lorraine pointed to a couple of markers on the threadbare carpet. "Could be the killer's, but they might belong to the man who found him."

"That was going to be my next question. Who found him?"

"A guy walking his dog. The dog ran in here and started licking the blood from the victim's wounds. The dog didn't respond to his recall, so the man was forced to step near the body to pull the dog away."

Sara grimaced. "Ugh… not good on all fronts. Is he still around?"

"He should be outside. I asked him to wait to speak with you."

Sara surveyed the room. "Do you think the killer has been staying here?"

"We're not sure who the victim is—correction, we know his identity but nothing more about him, so it's possible he might have been held prisoner here during his torture. Or he could have been abducted by the killer last night, tortured and killed within a few hours. I won't be able to tell you that, not until I examine the contents of the stomach to see what food or drink is in there."

"We'll get uniform to conduct house-to-house enquiries as normal, and after we've chatted with the witness, we'll track down the family, see if they can give us his final movements. There are food wrappers on the draining board, takeaway cartons, might be a few days' worth there."

Lorraine winked at her. "Well spotted. There's no electricity in the property." Lorraine gestured at the candles scattered around the room that were half burned. "Although there is water, so it is possible the killer had been using this place for a while."

"Again, we'll see what the neighbours have to say about that. I noticed there's a condemned sign on the door."

"It should be, this place is disgusting, even without a bloody corpse sitting in the middle of the room," Carla grumbled.

Sara approached Lorraine and held out her hand for the evidence bag. "Can we have his ID?"

Carla came to stand alongside Sara and jotted down the information. Then Sara got closer to the victim to observe the injuries he had sustained. She raised her hands in front of her and said, "Don't shoot me, it's only an observation."

"What is?" Lorraine asked.

"Give me a chance. At each of the crime scenes, yes, there's been dismemberment, but why do you think the heads were both still in place? I know that probably sounds an odd question, but isn't that usually the first part killers tend to hack off?"

Lorraine folded her arms, and her suit rustled as she placed a finger on her right hand against her cheek. "Good point, not something I've really given much consideration to as yet. If the victims were both tortured then I would say it's safe to assume that he inflicted the injuries while they watched."

"Sounds a reasonable assumption to me," Sara replied. "Have you checked the rest of the house? For more victims as well as extra evidence?"

"I had a brief hunt around; there's no one else in the property. No sign of bedding upstairs either, so if the killer was living here, he made sure he took all his personal effects with him," Lorraine said.

"And all his limbs are here? Nothing has been taken for a trophy?" Sara asked, casting her gaze over the crime scene.

"Yes, all present and correct. We're in the process of bagging it all up. I need to get on, ladies. Any other questions will have to wait until later."

Sara stood and took a step back to stand alongside Carla. "Gruesome, right?"

"And some. You know that lunch we forgot to have? I think I'm going to give it a wide berth today."

"Funny that, I was thinking the same. Come on, we'll

leave Lorraine and her team to it. Call me if anything significant turns up, Lorraine."

"You know I will."

Sara and Carla left the house. After depositing their suits in the evidence collection bag outside the front door, they sought out the witness. The man appeared to be understandably agitated. He was in his late fifties, with white hair and a small beard, dressed in jeans and a leather jacket that was wearing thin in several areas. At his feet lay a tan-coloured lurcher who jumped up as they approached.

Sara flashed her warrant card. "Hello, sir. Thank you for waiting to chat with us. I'm DI Sara Ramsey, the leading officer on the investigation, and this is my partner, DS Jameson."

"Pleased to meet you. It's dreadful, isn't it? Actually, it's far worse than that, but I can't summon up the right words to describe what I've seen without using swear words."

"I understand. Finding a dead body can come as a shock to the system."

"There's dead and there's *dead*. And I know I've never witnessed something as... well, depraved as that before in my life, and yes, I was in the navy, back in the day. Still never come across anything as gruesome as that before. What's the object of killing someone and mutilating them like that? It beggars belief, that's what."

"It does, sir. Would you mind telling us what happened?"

"Of course. Tommy here prefers to walk off lead, usually he's a good boy. But not today. Something led him up the garden path. I was a few feet behind him. I ran after him, but the door was open. He might have pushed it open, but I doubt it. Maybe it was the smell that drew him in, he's got a keen nose. Either way, it was such a disgusting thing to stumble across. I could have killed Tommy for licking the body. I called him away, but typical of a dog enjoying his meal, he refused to bloody budge. Not sure I'm ever going to be able to get rid of that image ever again. It's not his fault, I know that, but all the same… made me want to vomit seeing that man cut to shreds. Do you know who he is?"

"His ID was found inside the property. Are you from around here?"

"I am. I live a few roads over that way. Tommy and I walk past this house daily. I don't recognise him at all."

"Have you seen anyone living here? Or possibly visiting the property lately?"

He shook his head, and his mouth twitched as he thought. "I don't think so. I presumed this place was empty and that the council had condemned it. The inside was something from a bygone age. I'm not surprised it's on the condemned list. Have you asked the neighbours on either side?"

"That's next on our agenda. I didn't want to keep you waiting for too long, we've held you up long enough as it is."

"I'm fine. I'm not really, but I'd rather stick around and help you guys out here than have you turn up at my house, worrying the missus."

Sara smiled. "We won't keep you too long. And there was no one hanging around?"

"A couple of youngsters riding up and down on their bikes earlier, but no, that was all. I've been standing here wondering how those kids would have reacted if they'd found the body."

"It doesn't bear thinking about. Okay, that's all we need from you for now. Are you willing to give us a statement?"

"I don't mind, there's nothing further I can add."

"That's okay. We just need to make it official so we can use it as evidence when the case goes to court."

"Don't you have to find the person responsible first?"

"Yes, that's true. If you give us your name and address, we'll pass it on to a uniformed officer, and they'll make arrangements to see you at a convenient time within a few days."

"It's Steve Badger, I live at Fairview, Locksley Road, the house doesn't have a number. Don't ask, the wife wanted it that way, to stick two fingers up at the neighbours, I believe. She has a warped way of thinking, but we won't go there."

Sara smiled. "Thanks for the information, Mr Badger. You're free to go now."

"Thanks. Good luck with your investigation. This area used to be a safe place to live in. That's all changed in the past few years. Shocking, it is."

"We're doing our best to stamp out the more violent crimes in our society, Mr Badger."

"Oh, it wasn't a dig at you. No, far from it. It's as if a life means nothing these days. Deplorable, it is."

"I agree. Thanks for chatting with us. I'll give you one of my cards. If anything else should come to mind that you may have forgotten, don't hesitate to get in touch with me."

He smiled warmly. "I'll do that. You seem a very efficient young lady."

"Not sure about the young part, not these days."

"Get away with you. I'll let you get on. Come on, Tommy, and no shenanigans on the way home."

The man and his dog crossed the road and trotted past the SOCO's vehicle.

"Poor bloke. I bet he regrets walking his dog this way this morning," Carla said.

"Not half. Nice chap. Right, let's see what we can find out about the victim. Do you want to get Christine on it back at the station?"

Carla made the call while they walked back to the car. Sara had a fair idea where the victim's address was and started the engine.

Carla ended her call and confirmed she was going in the

right direction. "You're getting good at this. Christine is going to get back to us if she finds anything. Almost there. Take a left, and the house should be around the next corner."

And it was. They exited the vehicle, and Sara knocked on the door. No one answered, so they parted and went to see what each of the neighbours had to say. Fortunately, there was an elderly woman in at the house on the right. Sara produced her ID and offered it to the lady.

"DI Ramsey. Sorry to trouble you. I was wondering if you know your neighbours well." Sara pointed out the house she was referring to.

"Yes, Ned is such an adorable man."

"And his wife?"

She frowned. "Oh, he's not married. No plans on ever getting married, he told me. Had a few heartbreaks over the years, and he said he can't be bothered going through it all again."

"That's a shame. When was the last time you saw Ned?"

"Let me think. I didn't see him yesterday at all, which is unusual, I must say. Always stops to wave if he sees me. Teases me, he does." Her face lit up.

Sara didn't have the heart to tell the woman that her neighbour would be on his way to the morgue soon. "Does he have any family in the area?"

"Oh yes. He has a brother called Mick, he's an electrician. Always looking out for me, they are. Good boys. They lost their parents when they were both quite young."

"How sad. Does Mick have his own business or does he work for someone else?"

"He's self-employed. Wait a moment, I have his card here, I can let you have it. I have a pile of them, always keen to find him extra work, especially as the pair of them look after me so well."

"That would be fantastic, thank you."

Sara peered over the hedge at Carla and raised her thumb. Carla shrugged and walked away from the unanswered door and waited for Sara on the pavement outside the house she was attending.

"Here you go. He's very efficient. Not the type to rip people off like most of the tradesmen around these days."

"Good to hear. Thanks very much."

"You haven't said why you're here. I know I'm being nosey, but it will play on my mind all day if I don't ask."

"It's fine. We just need to speak with Ned about something he saw last week." A pimple erupted on Sara's tongue when the lie left her lips.

"Funny, he never mentioned it to me. Okay, I'm sure his brother will be able to help out."

"You've been extremely helpful. Enjoy the rest of your day."

"I will. I'm watching old black and white films today... ah, those were the days."

"Enjoy." Sara waved, and the woman closed the door.

Sara flicked the brother's card in her hand. "His brother is an electrician. I'll give him a call."

"You're going to tell him over the phone or go round there?" Carla glanced at the address. "It's only around the corner, on the edge of town."

"We'll go over there and have a chat, that is, if he's not out on a call."

SARA DREW up outside a commercial estate a few minutes later. Mick Foster's unit was right by the entrance. "We'll leave the car here, the exercise will do us some good."

"All of twenty feet. My fitness trainer will be super pleased with me," Carla replied sarcastically.

Sara poked her tongue out. Her stomach churning, she opened the door to the unit and stepped inside the building.

There was a woman in her forties sitting behind the desk, tapping away on a keyboard with headphones on. She glanced up from her work and paused her fingers. Removing the headphones, she asked, "Hello, can I help?"

Sara showed her ID and introduced herself. "Sorry to interrupt. I don't suppose Mick is around, is he?"

"As it happens, yes, he's out the back loading up the van for his next job. Want me to give him a shout for you?"

"That would be great, thanks."

"I'll be right back." She left her seat and exited the office. She returned a few moments later with a man in overalls. His hair was messed up and his face flushed. "This is Mick," the secretary said.

"Hi. What can I do for you?"

Sara smiled and flashed her warrant card. "I'm DI Sara Ramsey. Is it possible for us to have a chat in private, Mick?"

His gaze darted between Sara and Carla.

Sara added swiftly, "Sorry, and this is my partner, DS Carla Jameson."

"I don't care about your names, what I want to know is why you're here," he said, his gaze dropping onto Sara once more.

"It's personal, sir. Please, it would be better if we spoke with you alone."

He shrugged and ran his hands down his overalls. "You'd better come through to my tip of an office then. Please bear in mind that I'm out and about most days and barely spend any time in there."

"Don't worry. I promise we're not here to judge you on your housekeeping skills."

"Good, because I don't have any, neither here nor at home, my girlfriend can vouch for me on that one. In here."

91

He pointed to the only other door in the reception area. Sara and Carla followed him into a cluttered office. Reels of electrical cable and boxes of all sizes were on every surface available.

Mick stood next to his desk and crossed his arms. "Sorry, I can't offer you a seat. This place is a mess."

Sara shrugged. "Seriously, it's no problem. Mick, the reason we're here is to unfortunately break some bad news."

His brow furrowed, and he inclined his head. "About what?"

"Not what but who. I'm sorry to have to inform you that your brother's body was discovered this morning."

He paused for a moment or two, the shocking news sinking in. "His body? Are we talking about Ned here? I'm confused. You're telling me he's dead?"

Sara inhaled a steadying breath and filled him in. "I'm sorry. We've corroborated his ID which was found at the crime scene."

His hands dropped to his sides, then he wagged a finger. "No, wait, you said it so quickly I nearly missed it. 'Crime scene'. Tell me, how did he die?"

"We won't be able to give you a definitive answer until after the post-mortem has been carried out later on today."

"Why is a post-mortem necessary? Jesus, I can't get my head around the fact that he's dead, and here you are telling me he's going to be subjected to an autopsy—that is another name for it, isn't it?"

"It is. I'm afraid it's normal procedure when the victim has died in suspicious circumstances."

"What's suspicious about it? No, I believe I'm thinking clearly enough to understand what you mean. Are you saying he was murdered?"

Sara could clearly see the confusion in his expression, and her heart went out to him. "Yes, he's been murdered. I'm sorry, at this stage in the inquiry, we really can't tell you any more than that."

"Bullshit! How did he die? I have a right to know."

Sara swallowed down the touch of bile that had surfaced in her throat. "Okay, I can tell you something but not everything. It wouldn't be fair until we have the results from the pathologist to go on. Ned's body was found in a derelict house not far from his own home. He suffered injuries that indicate he was tortured before his death."

"Tortured? What type of injuries? I have a right to know, please tell me."

"Honestly, we can't go into detail, not just yet. It would be wrong of me to give you information that may turn out to be false."

"That's utter bollocks and you know it. All right, tell me why. Why was my brother mur... killed?"

"He was found less than an hour ago. The why remains perplexing. I fear we're not going to discover that until we begin interviewing people."

"And that's why you're here to see me, to interview me?"

"As well as sharing the sad news, yes. Are you up to answering our questions?"

"What questions? It depends on what they are and whether I know the answers or not. Jesus, he's really dead? This is so hard to take in."

"I'm sorry, I do understand how much of a shock this must be for you. We'll try to make this as painless as possible. Perhaps you can start by telling us when you last had any contact with your brother?"

Carla flipped open her notebook and poised her pen as he thought.

"It's Thursday now. He was on his way to the pub, he asked if I could join him, but I had to turn him down because I was working late, trying to finish a job that was running behind. I had to complete it on Tuesday because I had another job to start the next day. Being self-employed, you need to knuckle down and give up your social life a lot, I can tell you."

Sara nodded and smiled. "I can imagine. Did your brother mention where he was going for a drink?"

"Yeah, his local. The Lydal Arms. He went there as regular as clockwork."

"I see. Did he usually meet up with a group of friends or did he tend to drink alone?"

"A mixture of both. We all like our quiet times when we prefer to drink alone to contemplate life. But he's a regular at the pub. Odds are that someone would have had a drink with him that night."

"We'll pay the pub a visit after we've finished here. I have to ask if Ned had confided in you at all about any possible conflicts with anyone lately."

"Conflicts or arguments?"

"Either."

He paused and then shook his head. "I can't recall him saying anything. Are you telling me that someone who knew him did this?"

"It's unclear at the moment. The more questions we ask the sooner we're hopefully going to get our hands on the person responsible."

"When you arrest them, I'd like five minutes in a room with them, if that's allowed?"

"It's not. I can assure you, we'll throw the book at them. They won't be allowed to get away with this, not on my watch. I'm wondering if Ned would know a Ben Connor."

His frown deepened. "The name rings a bell, but I can't be sure."

"It's okay. If I give you my contact number, can I ask you

to ring me if it comes to you?" She handed him a card, and he took it.

"Sure."

"Did Ned have a girlfriend or significant other?"

"No. He's been steering clear of women for years. Too many bad experiences to last him a bloody lifetime. I told him he's going for the wrong types. He used to pick them up at pubs and nightclubs, and all the girls he went for seemed to latch on to him once he started flashing the cash and buying them drinks. He told me I was talking shite, though. I wasn't. It was true. He found out the hard way in the end."

"That's such a shame. When did he break up with his last girlfriend?"

"God, now you're asking. You know how quickly time flies, especially when you're up to your neck in work."

"Roughly?"

"At least a couple of years ago."

"Okay, I think that's too far back to worry about."

"Wait, why did you ask about that other chap? Ben, was it?"

Sara hesitated and then decided it couldn't do any harm, revealing the truth. "Unfortunately, Ben has also lost his life this week."

"What? Was he killed? Is that what you're telling me?"

"Yes. It's too early to be certain, but at this point we believe there are similarities to the crimes that we can't ignore."

"What does that mean? That you think they were killed by the same person?"

"It's a distinct possibility. Did Ned ever tell you that someone was following him?"

"No, he never mentioned it."

"Can I ask what he did for a living?"

"He was a carpenter. Our father always drummed it into us to get a trade behind us, told us that we'd never be short of cash. Never a truer word, especially during the pandemic. We were both chocka with work, both turning down extra jobs, whereas before the pandemic struck, it was hit and miss."

"What about someone he possibly let down? Did he have any arguments with any customers?"

"No, he really wasn't the type. He'd rather write the money off than get into a row with folks. I know everyone probably says this about someone when they're gone, but in Ned's case it's true. He was a decent chap who didn't deserve to go out this way. I'm gutted that I'll never sit down and have a pint with him again to discuss the football. It was hard enough when our parents died, we became closer after they passed. Relied on each other more, if you like. Now he's gone, too." He ran a hand over his face and hid his eyes. His shoulders trembled.

Sara felt awkward, unsure whether to approach him and offer him comfort or not. "Are you okay?"

He wiped his eyes on the cuff of his T-shirt and looked her in the eye. "If you want to know the truth, I don't think I'll ever be the same again. Not after this. Knowing that someone has intentionally killed him. How the hell does that happen? What gives someone the right to take another person's life just like that? Sick, it is, bloody sick."

"I agree. It's hard to fathom what goes on in someone's head at times such as this, when they rip families apart."

"I'm sincerely struggling to get my head around why they should choose Ned to kill. None of this makes sense at all. Could it be a case of mistaken identity? Could he have been plucked off the street? I suppose what I'm asking is, are you sure the killer intentionally went after him?"

"As yet, we're unsure of the facts. All we know is Ned's body was found in a condemned house, not far from his own. We don't know how long he'd been there, although the pathologist believes he was killed during the night."

"You can tell that?"

"It's surprising what the body can tell us after death. That's why we tend to keep an open mind about the cause of death until we have the results of the PM. It's no good surmising what might have happened only to have to eat our words and begin the investigation all over again. It's better to tread carefully from the start until we have the facts to hand."

"I get that. I apologise for coming down heavy on you."

Sara smiled again. "You didn't. You have a right to ask for the ins and outs of the case. In my defence, I would willingly give you all the details, but like I said, I'd much prefer to hold back and wait for the truth to be established. What type of mood was your brother in when you spoke to him?"

His chest swelled, and he exhaled the breath he'd sucked in. "He appeared to be his normal jokey self. No different from what I could tell. That's why this has come as a shock to me." He fell back against the wall. "What am I going to do without him? We weren't just brothers, we were best friends and confidants as well."

"Are you telling us that you didn't have any secrets?"

He bounced off the wall again. "No. We told each other everything, our deepest thoughts and secrets, and I swear, there was nothing in my brother's past that could possibly cause his death. I would tell you if there was."

"That gives us some indication of what we're dealing with then, although, I have to say that the way he died has led the pathologist to believe that maybe your brother knew his killer."

He shrugged. "I don't know what else to tell you, I'm sorry. This is all beyond me. Nothing seems logical right now."

"It's okay. We'll begin the investigation. You have my card.

97

Should you think of anything that might be relevant to the case, please get in touch."

"I will. You have my word."

He walked past them and opened the door. "Thanks for letting me know in person, I appreciate you coming to see me."

"I wouldn't have it any other way. Take care, Mick. Don't push yourself too hard in the circumstances."

"I'm not one for letting my customers down and I can't afford to get behind on my jobs."

"I completely understand. I want you to be aware that grief is a powerful emotion and can hit you when you least expect it."

"I'm aware but thank you for the warning."

Sara and Carla left the unit and walked back to the car.

"We're no further forward after speaking with him," Carla complained.

"As usual, I fear we're going to have to do this the hard way. Rarely do we get things handed to us on a plate, do we?"

"That's true. Are we going to the pub now?"

Sara opened the car doors. "Yep, let's see what they can tell us. At least we know he was around on Tuesday, so the likely scenario is that he got abducted then, either before the pub or afterwards, if he was already on his way there."

"Yep, sounds feasible."

THE PUB WAS dead when they got there. Two members of staff busy stocking up the shelves and no customers in sight.

The young barmaid came over to greet them. She pushed back a few stray hairs behind her ear and swiped her cheek. "How can I help?"

Sara flashed her ID. "Nothing to be alarmed about, we're

simply making enquiries. I don't suppose the owner or manager is around?"

"Oh, okay. Yes, Dale is out the back. I'll fetch him for you. Can I get you a drink while you wait?"

"He has you well trained. Keep the coppers onside if they show up, right?" Sara chuckled.

"Yep, how did you guess? I can fix you a coffee, it's no problem."

"Okay then, two white coffees with one sugar, thanks."

The barmaid gave a brief smile and dipped through the opening at the rear of the bar. Sara examined the area in the hope she would spot some cameras.

She nudged Carla and pointed at several dotted around, all angled in the direction of the bar. "Should be helpful."

A man wearing shorts and a tatty T-shirt appeared with the barmaid right behind him. "Hello, what can I do for you?"

The barmaid placed the two mugs of coffee in front of Sara and Carla.

"Thanks, you're very kind," Sara replied.

The barmaid returned to her job of filling the shelves.

"Can we talk here?" Sara asked.

Dale peered over his shoulder. "Yeah, they're fine, they know when to keep their mouths shut. What's going on?"

"I'm DI Sara Ramsey, the SIO in charge of a murder inquiry."

"What? And this has something to do with this pub?"

Sara noted the two members of staff staring at each other.

Dale looked behind him and said, "Ian and Charlie, take a break while we have a chat."

The couple left the bar area.

"No, it has nothing to do with the pub, not as far as we know. We're under the impression that the victim was heading this way on Tuesday evening. We're unsure whether he reached the pub that night or not and were wondering if you could confirm it."

"I'll do my best. Does the victim have a name?"

"He does." Sara hesitated slightly before telling him. "Ned Frost."

Dale took a step back then smashed both his fists against the counter. "Shit, are you winding me up?"

"No. I'm not in the habit of doing that, not during a serious investigation."

"Fuck. Yes, he was here on Tuesday. He's a regular here. Good bloke, he is... er, was. Sodding hell, I can't believe you're standing here telling me this."

"I take it he was a good friend of yours as well as being a customer, is that correct?"

"Yeah, he was the type to make friends easily. Always chatting away to someone in here."

"And what about Tuesday, was he talking to anyone in particular?"

"Yeah, me. It was a fairly quiet night. I was a staff member down, one of the girls rang in sick with bloody Covid, so I said I'd stand in for her. No big deal, it's my pub anyway. He sat at the bar all night, and we had a good catch-up while I served the other punters in between."

"And how did he seem to you?"

"His usual cheery self. No different to normal. Fuck... excuse my language, I can't believe he's dead. He was a good mate, long before I took over running this place."

"Did he get into any other conversations on Tuesday?"

"Yeah, general chitchat with others as they came up to the bar. A few people bought him a drink, to repay him—he was always putting his hand in his pocket, making sure others had a drink when he ordered one for himself."

"Did he seem uncomfortable in the slightest? As though he had something on his mind?"

"No. Not that I could tell. He left here after having a skin-ful. I offered to ring for a taxi. He waved the suggestion away, told me it would cost an arm and a leg and he was quite capable of staggering home on his own. Are you telling me he didn't get home?"

"We believe he might have been abducted en route."

"Oh, man, that's appalling. Why isn't it safe to walk the streets at night in this shithole of a town any more?"

Sara found herself lost for words and simply shrugged.

"I don't think it's that bad," Carla replied.

"You must be the only one then," Dale retorted harshly.

"I noticed you have cameras dotted around the bar area. Would it be possible to view the recordings from Tuesday night?" Sara asked. She picked up her mug and took a welcome sip if only to moisten her mouth which had become ultra-dry.

"What are you saying, that you don't believe me?"

"No, nothing like that at all. We would just prefer to see things for ourselves."

"Never in my wildest days have I ever had a cop coming in here doubting my bloody word."

Sara tutted. "That's not what I'm doing, Dale."

"Isn't it?"

"No. I apologise if that's the way it came across."

He huffed out a breath, turned away from the bar and muttered, "I'll get things set up and give you a shout. Why don't you enjoy your complimentary coffee in the meantime?"

Carla sniggered and sipped her drink. "That told you."

"Jesus, I didn't mean to upset him."

"Ah, but you did. You know how temperamental men can be when they feel challenged."

"You're not wrong," Sara whispered. She knocked back another couple of mouthfuls and stared at the opening behind the bar, willing Dale to appear. He didn't, not for a while.

Eventually, he returned to collect them. "Come round this way. I have the disc lined up for you to see." He gestured for them to walk around the bar and join him.

He showed them through to a tiny office, if you could call it that, as there was no desk in sight. The monitor sat on a pile of books, and Dale went about fiddling with the controls. The screen flickered to life, and Sara could see instantly how grainy the pictures were going to be.

"Dare I ask if you can get it any clearer?"

"I can't. It's not a state-of-the-art system, it's as old as this pub, and I think you should be grateful for what you're going to see."

That told me, again.

He played the disc, pointing out Ned and the odd person he spoke to throughout the next few hours. "As I told you, he sat at the bar, mostly on his own, and I kept him company during the evening."

"Just to reiterate, I didn't disbelieve you. What about the cameras outside? Anything there?"

He flicked around with the keys and brought up the cameras for outside. "Here we have everyone coming and going."

"And at what time did Ned arrive?" Sara asked. She took a step closer for a clearer view. If she thought the cameras inside were crap, it was nothing to what they were seeing on the ones outside.

"This is him arriving at eight-ten." Dale whizzed through the disc until another punter arrived, and then the next, only pausing at the end of the night when he saw Ned leaving the bar. "That's it, I thought he left at around ten-forty, but I wasn't sure enough to tell you."

"This is excellent. Would it be possible for you to run me off a copy?"

"Of all of it or only of Ned leaving?"

"All of it, if possible. Wait, can we watch where he goes until he disappears off the screen?"

"Sure."

Dale leant against the shelving unit beside him, and the three of them watched Ned stagger out of the car park and in the direction of his home. Disappointingly, there was no one else hanging around from what they could see. However, a few cars passed by around that time, but it was difficult to decipher any of the numberplates.

Dale got to work on duplicating the disc and told them to wait in the bar. Sara and Carla returned to where they were standing before and finished off their coffees.

"Touch and go there for a second," Carla leaned in and whispered.

Sara grinned. "Don't you love dealing with sensitive men? So tetchy!"

Carla covered her eyes with her hand. "You're hopeless."

"What this amounts to is that we're no further forward. I had hoped that we would have at least witnessed Ned's abduction in the car park. We didn't."

"Maybe forensics can help us out by analysing the cars that passed around the time he left. The images are really poor, so perhaps that's going to prove more difficult than we think."

"Worth a shot, though. Good call. We can drop the disc off on the way back to the station and call in to see Lorraine at the same time."

"Shit! Me and my big mouth. I know what that means."

"Yep, we might as well check on the PM while we're there."

"I knew it." Carla groaned.

Dale reappeared and slid a disc case across the bar to Sara. "That's all you saw out back."

Sara picked up the case and smiled at him. "Thanks so much. We really do appreciate all your assistance. Sorry for the misunderstanding."

He gave a brief nod and turned his back on them.

"I think that's our cue to leave," Sara murmured out of the corner of her mouth.

CHAPTER 5

*S*ara parked the car outside the forensics' lab and, along with a very reluctant Carla, entered the building.

A man in a white coat appeared once the bell sounded on the door. He smiled, recognising them both. "Hi. What can I do for you today, Inspector?"

"I have a favour to ask."

"Shoot, what do you need?"

Sara tapped the disc against her palm. "I have very grainy CCTV footage that I need tweaking. How are you fixed?"

"Hmm… let me think. How about if I get it back to you by late afternoon tomorrow?"

"That would be excellent." Sara handed over the disc and said, "Any chance you can make a duplicate copy now, enabling us to show the rest of the team what we've discovered?"

"It shouldn't be a problem. I'll be back in a couple of minutes."

The man took the disc and walked a few paces down the hallway to the first room on the right. Sara was tempted to join him but managed to suppress the urge. Instead, she nervously paced the area, much to Carla's annoyance.

"Stand still, you're doing my head in going around in circles. It's making me feel dizzy."

"Sorry. You know what I'm like, I can't keep still for long."

"No shit! Ah, here he is now."

Sara spun around and smiled at the technician whose name she had temporarily forgotten. He handed her the disc case with a smile.

"There you go, all copied. I'll do my best to get the other disc back to you tomorrow. Of course, if something urgent arises in the meantime, that will need to take priority."

"I understand. Do you know if Lorraine is around?"

"Yes, she's carrying out the post-mortem on the latest victim. I'm sure she won't mind if you go through."

"Thanks, we might as well drop by and see her while we're here."

"Feel free. You know the way."

"We do. Do you need us to sign in?"

"You'd better, to be on the safe side, in case there's a fire while you're here."

"Christ, don't say that."

They walked over to the reception desk, and he pulled out the visitors' book for both of them to sign. Then he bid them farewell, leaving them to find their own way to the mortuary, which wasn't a problem as they'd visited it hundreds of times before over the years.

Lorraine's office was empty, as expected, so they carried on down the corridor to the autopsy suite which Lorraine preferred to call her 'theatre', where she performed miracles with the dead bodies that came her way, interpreting the more intricate details of their deaths which ultimately aided the investigation teams.

She looked up and waved a bloody gloved hand at them. Then she shouted, "Do you want to come in and join me?"

"Not particularly," Carla muttered beside Sara.

Sara dug her partner in the ribs. "Get away with you. Where's your sense of adventure gone?"

"Umm… it's packed a bag and set off on its own."

Sara chortled. "Silly bugger. Come on, let's get togged up." She raised a thumb at Lorraine and held up three fingers. "We'll be three minutes."

Lorraine nodded and got back to what she was doing.

Sara and Carla entered the changing room and appeared wearing fetching greens and white rubber shoes.

"This outfit does wonders for my street cred," Carla grumbled.

"I think you look beautiful in anything and everything, unlike me."

"Jesus, fishing for compliments at a time like this. You never cease to amaze me."

Sara rolled her eyes. "I wasn't, but I doubt if you're gonna believe me."

They reached the door to the autopsy suite. Out of courtesy, Sara knocked on the portal window and waited for Lorraine to give them the all-clear to enter.

"Welcome, ladies. Was I expecting you? I can't remember if we discussed your attendance on this one or not."

"Not. We had to drop something off at the lab so thought we might as well call in to see how the PM is going."

"As you can see, I've not long begun. I was delayed. I had another PM to squeeze in, a fifteen-month-old baby who went through the windscreen. The mother is in critical condition. Only time will tell if she's going to make it or not."

"How dreadful. Makes you stop and think when you hear a baby losing its life before it has really begun," Sara said, a hand squeezing her heart.

"How do you deal with something like that, Lorraine?" Carla said, clearly choked.

Lorraine let out a sigh and shrugged. "I find myself switching off the emotional part of my brain and concentrating on dealing with the facts."

"And the facts are?" Sara asked.

"That the child wasn't correctly fastened in the rear seat, and when the mother applied her brakes, the child went through the windscreen."

"And how did the accident occur?"

"The mother took a corner too fast and skidded on the wet road. She ended up hitting some scaffolding. Luckily, there were several builders in the area. They secured the structure as best they could and tugged the mother out of the vehicle, but it was too late for the baby, she was already dead."

"And the father?"

"I believe she's a single mother," Lorraine replied. She snapped at the cuff of her right glove. "Don't, I need to move on, I can feel the emotion rising every time I think of the guilt that woman is going to have to live with for the rest of her life."

"So depressing," Sara agreed. "Okay, I'm sorry I asked what the delay was now. That's spoilt my day, even if it hadn't been spoilt before."

"Let's not dwell on things that are out of our hands. Right, I've assessed all the external injuries. I believe the limbs were removed with a general saw. His fingers were broken with an instrument gripping the digits, so I'm thinking along the lines of pliers."

"Makes sense. His brother told us he was a carpenter, so maybe the killer used his own tools to torture him with," Sara suggested.

"All well and good, but he was on a night out, he wasn't carrying a bag when he entered the pub," Carla added.

Sara nodded. "I'll give you that one."

"Can I get on?" Lorraine asked.

Sara grinned. "Don't mind us. Any idea what the COD is?"

"Cause of death is likely to be that he either bled out from the multiple injuries or maybe he suffered a heart attack because of the added stress his body was going through at the time. I won't know if that's the case until I complete a thorough examination of his organs."

"We've dropped the CCTV footage off for your guys to enhance for us, they're grainier than a Pathé News clip."

"That bad, eh?" Lorraine laughed. "Did you pick up anything of substance from the clip?"

"Nope. The landlord had already told us that he spent most of the night chatting with Ned, and the footage backed that up from what we could tell. Ned also spoke to a few of the other regulars in between Dale, the landlord, serving, but nothing of significance. We checked the cameras outside the pub, spotted Ned staggering home but, again, there was nothing untoward going on in the car park," Sara relayed the information, her gaze firmly fixed on the Y-section incision that Lorraine had made in the corpse before they had arrived.

"Don't forget the few cars that passed the pub after he left," Carla reminded her.

"Which is why we dropped the disc off. If we can figure out where he was abducted then that's when I believe the investigation will take off. Until then, we have absolutely nothing to go on."

"It's a tricky one for sure. A bit like the first victim," Lorraine proposed. "I have no doubt in my mind that the crimes are connected. We have similar MOs, but the instruments of torture are slightly different. Is that intentional? Did the killer want us to piece the puzzles together or was he sloppy?"

"It would be nice to find out, once we've arrested the bastard. What we need to know is if the two men were targeted for a specific reason. We asked Ned's brother if Ned knew Ben Connor. He said he did, from what he could remember, but couldn't go into detail of how he knew him," Sara said.

"Might be worth asking Tess before the day is out," Carla suggested.

Sara nodded. "I'll give her a call when we get back to the station. That is, if she doesn't refuse to take my call."

Lorraine's head tilted to the side. "Why should she do that?"

"Because of the grief she's experiencing," Sara stated. Then she caught Carla shaking her head. "What's wrong?"

"Grief or the effects of the pummelling she received from Ben before he died?" Carla asked.

Sara shifted uncomfortably on the spot. "It doesn't feel right condemning the man now that he's dead, does it?"

Carla hitched up a shoulder. "Why not? It's the truth."

"May I remind you that's not what his parents told us," Sara replied, unsure why she felt the need to stick up for Ben, particularly if he had abused Tess.

"You can discuss the whys and wherefores later, ladies. I need to get on with the PM now."

"Don't mind us," Sara said.

Lorraine dug around in the chest opening and then took a scalpel from the silver tray beside her and removed the heart. She placed it under a bright lamp to assess it in detail and then shook her head. "My first inclination is to say that the heart was intact. No obvious sign of trauma."

"So he bled out?" Sara asked. "The question is, did he die

in front of the killer or did the killer leave the property once he knew Ned was on his way out?"

"I should think there are a lot of unanswered questions with these two cases. I'm doing my very best to help you ladies out, but from what I can tell, the killer definitely knows how to cover his tracks. We've yet to find any clear evidence or DNA from the killer at either of the scenes."

"That's not welcome news at all, Lorraine. Wait, even though we reckon he was at the property where Ned was found at least a few days before?"

Her pathologist friend shrugged. "Yep, believe me, we're doing our utmost to find something, so don't you give up on us just yet."

"Don't worry, we won't, you're all we've got."

THE PM TOOK another hour or more to complete with no real conclusion at the end of it. Sara and Carla left the mortuary feeling down and inept.

"I hate it, feeling this bad so early on in an investigation," Carla said.

Sara slowed down the vehicle and slipped into the station's car park. She switched off the engine and rested her head back. "I was thinking the same. It's always the not knowing that screws with your head. Two murders within a few days of each other. Two young men, one with a dubious background, if Tess is to be believed, and the other a decent chap, earning a trade as a carpenter who appeared to be well liked." She raised her hands upright and dropped them into her lap. "Where do we go from here?"

"I wish I could tell you," Carla said in a defeated tone.

Sara unhitched her seatbelt and tore open the car door. "I know one thing, sitting here being on a downer isn't going to do us much good, is it?"

"You're right. Let's get down to the real work and find this bastard before he adds to the number of victims lying in the mortuary."

On the way back, they had stopped off at the baker's and collected lunch for the team. Sara grabbed the bag from the back seat, and they headed into the station.

"Everything all right, Jeff?" Sara asked the desk sergeant who seemed a tad perplexed.

"Yes, ma'am. Busy arranging the house-to-house for you, but the team seems to be a bit thin on the ground today for some reason."

Sara smiled. She had enough on her plate to contend with, without getting caught up in someone else's dilemmas. "I'm sure you'll have it all figured out soon enough."

"I will. Don't worry."

They continued their journey up to the incident room to find the team all hard at it.

"We took a gamble and presumed you hadn't had lunch," Sara announced. "You'll have to sort out who wants what between you. They didn't have much left to choose from by the time we showed up."

"Which is yours?" Christine asked.

"I'm really not bothered. You guys choose first, and I'll have what's left, how's that?"

Carla chose a ham and cheese on white bread and then made her way over to the drinks station to prepare the coffee. Sara joined her as the rest of the team chose from the sandwiches on offer.

Once everyone was sorted, they gathered around to discuss the investigation over lunch. "I know we haven't discovered much yet, but hopefully that will all change now that the pathologist has confirmed the two cases are linked. Therefore, we need to keep digging for anything the two men might have had in common. Mick Frost told us that he knew Ben Connor and so did his brother. I think that's where we should start."

"What about Ben's girlfriend, Tess? Are we dismissing her possible involvement now?" Craig took a chunk out of his sandwich.

"I think we should leave it on the backburner for now. Which reminds me, I need to give her a call, see if she can share anything about the victims' relationship, other than the fact they just knew each other."

"Sounds mysterious," Jill said. "Maybe they were hiding a dark secret between them which eventually led to their deaths."

Sara mulled the idea over and nodded. "It's not outside the realms of possibility. Let's sit on all conjecture for now and stick with the facts. We're going to need to dig deep into their backgrounds. Get me a list of friends and perhaps exes from their social media if they're the type to use it."

"Who doesn't these days?" Carla added.

"That's true. I'll leave it with you and call Tess from my office." Sara picked up her mug and what was left of her sandwich and transferred to the privacy of her office to make the call. She looked up Tess's number and dialled it while she nibbled on a lump of cheese that had toppled out of her sandwich.

"Hello, Tess speaking."

"Hi, Tess. This is DI Sara Ramsey, we met a few days ago."

"Yes, I remember. Do you have any news for me?"

"Not regarding Ben's death, unfortunately. What I'm calling about is to see what you can tell me about Ned Frost. I believe he was a friend of Ben's, is that correct?"

"Yes, Ben knew him. Did Ned have something to do with Ben's death?"

"No, not at all, at least we don't think so. Sadly, Ned's body was found this morning in a condemned house."

"He's dead? Oh my. How awful."

"It is. Which is why I'm reaching out to you. We've spoken to Ned's brother, and he mentioned that Ned and Ben were friends, but he wasn't too sure how well they knew each other. I wondered if you might be able to fill me in with some details."

"I can try. They used to play snooker together at the club in town. Not that often. I suppose work got in the way for both of them occasionally, what with Ned being self-employed. I think that pissed Ben off now and again. Ned would make arrangements to have a game of snooker only for him to let Ben down at the last minute if an emergency job came his way. I believe Ned was the ultimate professional, who always went the extra mile for his customers. How sad that he's gone. I really liked him, not that I saw that much of him. Do you think the same person who killed Ben went out and killed Ned as well?"

"It's looking likely, yes. Although, it's still early days."

"Are you telling me you don't have any leads yet?"

"I am. We're only a few days into the investigation, but from what we can gather, the killer is on the ball. So far, our initial examinations have failed to find any DNA at either of the scenes."

"Does that happen a lot?" Tess asked, her voice faltering slightly.

"On the rare occasion. We're doing all we can to find something, you have my word on that."

"I'm glad you're not giving up. You hear so many scare stories regarding the police where crimes have remained unsolved for years."

"Don't worry, my team and I have no intention of adding to the statistics of the unsolved crimes in this country. That's never on the agenda for us. We're like the Mounties in that respect, we always get our man."

114

Tess let out a sigh. "That's a relief. I have to admit that I've been sitting here wondering if you would ease off."

"Sorry, but that's not in my nature. We will press ahead with both investigations. Hopefully, something will crop up soon that will lead us to the killer. In the meantime, don't be afraid to give me a call if your confidence wavers a little. I hope this conversation has overcome any fears you may have had. I can categorically say we're doing our very best to find the person responsible for Ben's death, and now Ned's, of course."

"Thank you, that has reassured me. Was there anything else, Inspector?"

"No. That's all. You have my number if you should need it."

"I do. Good luck with the rest of your investigation. I still feel very numb about the revelation."

"I'm sure. Please try and remain positive. I won't rest until we've found the perpetrator, neither will my team."

Sara ended the call and attempted to finish the rest of her sandwich but no longer had the stomach for it. She threw it in the bin beside her. The same couldn't be said for her coffee which she finished off in one large gulp. Then she picked up her pen and sought out a clean piece of paper on which she jotted down some notes about the two crimes. Over to the left she wrote Tess's name and circled it a few times. After speaking to the woman and hearing how 'well' she sounded, Sara wondered, not for the first time, if there was more going on with Tess than she first realised.

Only time will tell if my gut is right about her. Plodding on.

CHAPTER 6

*H*e found the Range Rover quite comfortable to sleep in compared to his previous digs. Owen had managed to grab a shower at the local gym, where he'd been a member for the last five years, so there was nothing odd about him going there, nothing that would raise any suspicions anyway. After a general workout on the various muscle-defining and enhancing equipment, he plunged under a cold shower to relieve the lingering stress surging through his veins. He had mistakenly thought that ridding the world of two people who had treated him badly in the past would cure him, but it hadn't. Which had left him reeling, wondering if anything would succeed in making him better, or whole again.

Owen parked the vehicle in a space close to the house and settled down to observe. All the time his mind was in turmoil, going back and forth between the torture he'd recently inflicted and what had led him to be here today.

He sat upright; the front door had opened. His heart fluttered and then thundered wildly. There she was. Looking as beautiful and serene as ever. She didn't seem too bad. He thought she might be devastated after losing her boyfriend, but she seemed fine to him. She walked up the street, towards him. *Wait, is she limping?* He pulled the hood around his face and snuck a peek at her as she passed. His anger growing tenfold. *Is that a black eye?* All he wanted to do was wrap his arms around her, tell her he was there for her and that he would never let another man lay his hands on her again. He would protect her. Do everything in his will to make her world right. For her to be happy and live without fear once more. But he would need to wait, sensing the time wasn't right, not yet.

Starting up the engine, he watched through his wing mirror as she turned into the next street. Mixed emotions clawing at every nerve and muscle. He clenched his fists a few times and then selected Drive on the shaft. The vehicle eased out of the parking space and crept along the road to the junction at the end. He could see her. Checking the rear-view mirror and finding the road clear behind him, he remained in the same spot for a few moments until Tess crossed the road and headed towards the town centre.

The Range Rover crawled down the street and again paused at the top. He momentarily freaked out, unable to see her, and then he let out a relieved breath as he spotted the red collar on her jacket in the distance. Owen drove into the main thoroughfare, got caught up in the traffic and lost her again. Furious, he beeped the car in front to get a move on. The driver gave him the finger. Had he not had his mind elsewhere, he would have torn out of the car and given the driver a good hiding. However, upon reflection, that would have drawn attention to him in the busiest part of the city.

Instead, once he'd driven through the lights, he parked the car in the underground Tesco car park and set off on foot up the high street, hoping he would remember the shops she used to visit when they had been together.

His stomach muscles clenched the longer he went without laying eyes on her. He thought he spotted her once, took off in a trot to catch up with her, but he'd been mistaken. It turned out to be a woman in her sixties wearing a similar jacket. *It looks better on Tess than this old cow.*

He peered around the next corner, where all the eateries were situated, the street traders and the cafés surrounding the marketplace. It was heaving. Then he remembered Tess always preferred going to M&S for a coffee when she was in town. Maybe he should check there first.

The escalator was jam-packed, and it chugged up to the first floor under the extreme weight of all the customers too lazy to take the stairs that ran alongside it. *So much for social distancing, or has that gone out of the window these days?* He'd always practiced social distancing as far back as he could remember, hating everyone who came into his personal space unless they were invited. Tess had always been the exception to the rule.

There she was, up ahead, sitting at the table, buttering a scone. He bought a coffee and an Eccles cake and sat at one of the tables close to the exit, aware she would need to pass him on the way out. He'd make his move then. After paying the lady at the till, he collected a serviette, sugar and a spoon from the small counter on the right and continued on his journey to his carefully selected table, keeping his head low in case she turned his way and spotted him.

Nibbling on his cake—it had been a while since he'd remembered to eat anything—he took several sips of his coffee. His gaze never leaving the love of his life. He was conscious he'd need to play it cool with her. That's why he had chosen such a public place to step out of his comfort zone and say hello.

She tidied up her table, placing the empty plate and the cup and saucer on the tray then slid it away from her. *Is she leaving now?* Tess paused to check her phone. She had always been addicted to social media. A few minutes later, she tucked her phone into her handbag and rose from the table.

He prepared himself and swallowed down the acid burning his throat. *What's wrong with me? I'm acting like a love-struck teenager on his first date. Here she comes.* He kept his head bowed and then raised it when she came within a few feet of him. "Tess, oh wow, fancy meeting you here."

Tess halted by his side, and their gazes locked. Emotion swam in her eyes along with the sudden tears that had materialised.

"Owen, what are you doing here?"

He grinned. "Umm… being naughty, adding to my waistline, having a sneaky cake and coffee."

She glanced at the tray and the contents left on the table. "All alone?"

"Yes. What about you? It's good to see you again, Tess."

"Yep, alone, collecting my thoughts over a scone and cream. It helps to put life back into perspective, doesn't it?"

"It does. How's life been treating you lately?" he dared to ask, a sudden rush of desire whooshing through every limb, an effervescence bubbling in his stomach.

She puffed out her cheeks, and her shoulders slumped. "I've had better weeks. Sorry, I'm in a hurry, I have somewhere I need to be. I just nipped in for a quick coffee and cake because I forgot to eat at lunchtime. It was lovely seeing you again after all this time."

He pushed his cup and saucer away and stood. "I'm finished here. I'll walk out with you, if that's okay?"

She shuffled her feet, making him wonder if he'd come on too strong and had overstepped the mark.

But in the next moment, she nodded. "Okay, that would be nice."

They walked through the ladies' underwear department.

He resisted the urge to release a childish giggle, fully aware that Tess wouldn't be seen dead in any of this gear. As far as he could remember, she had excellent taste in choosing matching underwear. He'd even bought her some himself, at the beginning of their relationship, when they were lusting after each other, from none other than Victoria's Secret. His crotch twitched at the thought of her modelling it for him and what it had led to that warm summer evening.

"Did you hear me?" she threw over her shoulder at the top of the stairs.

"Sorry, no. I was miles away. What did you say?"

"I asked where you're living now."

"Ah, right. I'm staying at a friend's house for a little while. I've put my name down for a new build, but it's going to take a few months before it's ready."

"How exciting. Where?"

Damn, he hadn't thought about that. He wracked his brain, trying to think of a new-build site he'd driven past in the last week or so, but nothing came to mind. *Shit!* "Out in the sticks, in one of the villages north of the city. You're going to think I'm a right numpty; the name of the village has escaped me, sorry. It must be the thrill of seeing you again, my mind is in a daze."

"Oh, I see. Well, not to worry. I'm over the moon for you. A word of warning, though, I've heard so many scare stories regarding new builds. They're flying up all over the place, too fast and low quality according to some articles I've read on the internet. Just be careful and make sure you do your research into the company selling it before you sign on the dotted line. Gosh, listen to me, I had no right lecturing you like that, just ignore me."

"Lecturing me? I didn't take it as that at all. You were just looking out for a dear friend, weren't you?"

"I suppose so. It's better to be armed with the facts rather than be hit by a costly mistake a few months or years down the line."

"I'll have a rethink and definitely take your advice on board. You always were a really practical girl. Ouch, sorry, did that sound condescending?"

Tess's cheeks coloured up under his gaze. "Not at all. Yes, I've always been one to analyse a situation thoroughly before jumping in feet first, which generally hacks men off. But we won't go there."

He bit down on the words threatening to emerge, asking her about where she'd got her black eye and limp from, but he avoided the question in case it brought his anger to a head. Instead, he smiled warmly and asked, "What about you? Where are you living?"

By this time, they had reached the bottom of the stairs and were standing by the entrance, getting in the other customers' way. The shop was the busiest it had been for a couple of years, now that the restrictions had been fully lifted and life was back to what everyone considered to be normal after living through two years of hell on earth.

"Heck, that's another thing I need to consider. The list is never-ending."

He frowned, confused by her response, and queried, "Sorry, have I missed something?"

"No, I just never told you. It's still too raw to mention. I've... no, I can't. I'm sorry, I have to go now, Owen. Please forgive me, it's been lovely catching up with you. Good luck with the move, and don't forget to research thoroughly before you do the deal." She turned to walk towards the door.

"Wait, Tess. Come back, don't go like this. Are you sure you're all right? Was it something I did or said that has upset you?"

"No, I apologise if I gave you that impression. Forgive

me," she repeated. "I have a lot on my plate right now. I need to go."

Then she strode through the doors and out of his life, again. He stood there, watching her until she became a pinprick in the distance. He thumped his thigh with every step she took.

An elderly woman tapped him on the shoulder and asked, "Are you okay?"

"What? Yes. Of course I am. What's it to you? Keep your bloody nose out, you old bag."

"Hey, don't talk to her like that," a man twice his age shouted, coming to the old woman's defence.

Owen took a few quick steps towards the man and watched him shrivel back into the small gathering that had developed around the old woman. "Shit! Fuck off the lot of you. You need to keep your nose out of my business."

Beyond the crowd, the security guard was heading their way. Not wanting to get into yet another confrontation that might get him arrested, Owen marched out of the store and made his way back to the car park. *Maybe I'll catch up with Tess, if I'm quick.*

Upping his pace, he bumped into several of the shoppers in his eagerness to catch up with the woman he loved. To no avail. Disappointment mixed with anger tore through him, and the recriminations filtered through his mind. *Why did I let her leave like that? Why did I ever let her go in the first place? All of this could have been avoided. Why did she fall out of love with me when I gave her everything I had and more? Why...? Why...? Why...?* Dozens more unfinished questions were on the tip of his tongue but were never asked and consequently added to his confusion. There was only one way to rid himself of the emotions wrangling within—to go on the prowl again.

The Range Rover stood out loud and proud above the rest

of the cars parked in the underground area. It had been his most successful moment in years, stealing the car. It had buoyed his mood and given him something to cling on to. Given him the perception that he was capable of obtaining the unattainable, if he put his mind to it. He jumped in the car, and the tyres squealed their objection as he left the car park and drove up the slight incline to the street outside.

He headed out of town and, in need of a nap parked up in a lay-by. Seeing Tess and experiencing the sensations that had arisen had scarred him emotionally, leaving him feeling wrung out. He switched off the engine, pulled his hood up to give him extra comfort and drifted off to sleep. She cropped up in his dream, never far from his thoughts. In the dream she was wearing a long floaty dress that was billowing and swaying in the breeze. She ran barefoot through the long grass of the meadow up on the Malvern Hills. They had visited the area quite a lot when they had been dating. Exhausted, she lay on the grass beside him, swivelled sideways to place her head on his lap and chewed on a long blade of grass, peering through the haze of the sunshine and smiling up at him.

Then the dream turned on its head, and he was reliving the day Tess had finished with him. He had come home late from the pub and tried it on with her, groping her in the bed beside him. She had distinctly said no, but he had forced himself upon her. He had regretted his actions the second he had ejaculated and she had dashed out of the bedroom and into the bathroom. He had knocked on the door after hearing her being sick. Why had he done it? Selfish bloody bastard.

He woke with a start and glanced around him. It was pitch-black outside, no streetlights around this area to highlight the car. Owen smashed a fist onto the dashboard. "No wonder she couldn't wait to get away from me today. She looked uncomfortable several times throughout the conversation. I shouldn't be surprised by that. Why did I have to take her like that? Up until then we'd had a fantastic relationship but, with a blink of the eye, one drunken night's calamity had torn that apart in an instant. Why?"

He repeatedly shook his head, recapping the strained months after that disastrous evening. He'd ruined any trust she'd ever had in him, for what? To get his end away in a quick fumble. Finally, after weeks of her shrinking before his eyes and retreating into her shell, she'd plucked up the courage to tell him it was over between them. Seeing the distress she had been through in the few months since he'd... taken her against her will... he didn't have it in him to try and talk her around, so he'd merely walked away from her and the life they had shared together for over five years. He was at fault, it was his responsibility to right the wrong and let her get on with her life. He had regularly kept an eye on her. His first port of call, coming back from a stint with the army, had always been to stop by the house, to see how she was getting on, if only from a distance.

One day, he'd returned and was frantic when he discovered she had moved out of the house she had rented. He'd searched the city high and low to locate her. Visited her old haunts, dropped by her place of work, only to be told she had moved on, but they couldn't tell him where. Fearing that he'd never lay eyes on her again had paralysed him for days. What would he do without her? Although she wasn't with him as such, he had always had her within reaching distance, if he needed her. Now, she was gone.

Then one day he was walking through the park when he spotted her, arm in arm with Ben Connor. It angered him to see the way she peered up at him adoringly. She had done the same to Owen once upon a time, or had she? Had she ever been as happy with him as she was with Ben? Doubts clouded his mind. He'd followed them back to the home they shared. Settled into the shadows and watched with interest what went on inside the house. He became obsessed. Going away on manoeuvres and returning to pick up where he'd left off, keeping the pair of them under observation for hours, even days, on end. Until a few days ago, when something had triggered the anger inside. He knew exactly what that was. He'd had the house under surveillance, as usual, and was watching Tess and Ben shouting at each other. She went upstairs, and he ran after her. She had screamed at one point. Although he wasn't sure why, he assumed that Ben had struck her. Though, he'd had no proof of that likelihood until today, once he'd seen the bruise covering her eye. She had tried to disguise it with makeup, but the stronger purples and black were still there for all to see.

His actions had been vindicated. Killing Ben had been justified. He didn't deserve Tess, no one did, except Owen. He'd screwed up once, but he would never allow that to happen again. All he needed to do now was to convince her that he'd changed. That he was no longer the angry man who had once violated her, turned a deaf ear when she had pleaded with him to stop.

He had changed, well, he was getting there. He would be fully cured in the next few days, once he'd rid this world of all the people who had wronged him over the years. Then, and only then, would he be free to live a stress-free life, with Tess. He had recognised something in her eyes during their conversation earlier. He was confident she still had feelings for him. Why else would she have stopped to chat with him? What he hadn't anticipated, though, was her running out on him the way she had. Why was that? Had he come on too strong? Despite telling himself to hold back and to take things easy?

The angry exchange with the small crowd that had taken

place after she had left came hurtling back to him. The rage erupted within, and there was only one way he knew to correct it. He started the engine and shifted in the driver's seat to find a more comfortable position before setting off. He visualised the notes he'd made about his next target and glanced down at the clock. It was almost eight; he knew exactly where the man would be at this time of night. At the gym, his local gym. He drove to the location and parked in the street, outside the car park, away from any possible cameras, and waited for Lipsey to appear. His bag on the back seat, his equipment to hand, ready for the onslaught.

He had around an hour to play with before Lipsey surfaced from the gym. He spent the time going over what he wanted to say to the man who had been his nemesis for years, fighting alongside him in the army. Andrew Lipsey was his equal, the same rank as him, but you wouldn't think so, not by the way he'd spoken to him. Always keen to put him down. Bullying him just to get his kicks in front of their colleagues. Well, that was about to end tonight. Owen would be the one having the last laugh, at Lipsey's expense.

As the time approached, he reached into the back seat and opened the zipper of his holdall. Withdrawing the knife, he tucked it up his right sleeve. It felt comfortable to have it close to him. His gaze was drawn to the entrance of the gym. The car park was full. Up until now, he had avoided using the place around this time, knowing how busy it could get. People came and went. Each time the main door opened he sat forward, only to recline again when it turned out to be a false alarm.

Finally, ten minutes after the time he usually left the gym, Lipsey surfaced and, after chatting to a few guys who were on their way in, he left the car park. Owen hopped out of the Range Rover parked where it was and set off on foot, keeping a reasonable distance behind his target and sticking to the shadows, his hood in place, acting as a shield. He followed him through the alley and across the park, choosing to walk on the grass and close to the shrubs and trees, thus avoiding the crunch of the gravel where possible, just in case Lipsey turned around and saw him.

It was crucial for Owen to time the attack with precision. He was determined to strike while they were still hidden from the street but within close proximity to the exit for Lipsey to be found fairly soon after the attack.

He sensed Lipsey was about to peer over his shoulder, and Owen darted behind an old oak tree. He peeked around the trunk and watched the man get underway again. It was almost time now. Another few steps and he'd make his move. His perfect eyesight had adjusted to the dark, and he peered through the trees ahead of him. If he upped his pace, even sprinted, he would be ahead of Lipsey in no time, then he could jump out on him, catching him unawares, and do the deed.

A few dead branches lay in his path, fatalities of the storm they had experienced only the previous week. He flew over them with all the ease of a gazelle, keeping his eye on Lipsey to the left of him. Up ahead, he could make out an opening in the shrubs. He would surge ahead and lie in wait for Lipsey to come up alongside him. His pulse quickened with every step he took. His pace never faltered and, before long, he found himself at the opening, slightly ahead of Lipsey.

Pushing from the trees, he stood with his feet apart. Lipsey gasped, an expression of confusion clouding his features, until the hatred seeped into his eyes.

"Well, well, well, who do we have here then? Owen Silver, a man of few talents with the charisma of a beetle. What brings you here?"

"Fond of spouting your mouth off, ain't ya, Lipsey? Look

around you. In case you hadn't noticed, there's no one else around for you to impress with your evil condemnations."

"I only speak the truth. You're an utter waste of space. You've put more lives at risk on duty than all of the others put together. I just made a point of showing the commanding officers what they neglected to see. I'm glad you're out of the army now, the timing couldn't have been better. The whole regiment was relieved to see the back of you, not just me."

Owen took a step towards Lipsey and sneered, "I've had your back on more occasions than I care to remember. Saved your life more than once, and this is how you repay me. Why? Were you embarrassed to find yourself in such a position? Thought of yourself as the big I am to go along with that epic fucking mouth of yours? You're the *waste of space*. All mouth and no action. I saved your life when you chose to run from the enemy, took out that Taliban fighter when he had you in his sights and you ran for the hills. If I hadn't followed the pair of you up that mountain and taken him out, you frigging wouldn't be here today, arsehole. We went back to camp, and you made up some cock-and-bull story about killing the bastard with your bare hands, and the other morons believed every word that tripped out of your mouth."

"I don't recall it being quite like that, but each to their own."

Lipsey's refusal to admit he was in the wrong infuriated Owen even more. "You're a bastard. Instead of thanking me, you set out to ridicule me in front of the others. What kind of person does that make you?"

"The men all believed me rather than you, whom they despised. Who was likely to be telling the truth? Not you. They hated being in the same room as you, sleeping in close quarters next to you. Why? Because everyone perceived you as being a weirdo. Not all there up here." Lipsey prodded his temple and glared at him.

Owen grinned. "Is that so? Maybe they had a point. I suppose nowadays I might be classed as a weirdo in their eyes. Living in a Range Rover while prowling the street for people to knock off. Yes, that's exactly what weirdos do, isn't it?"

"What are you talking about? Have you finally lost your marbles, man?"

"Possibly. Why do you think that is?"

Lipsey hitched up his left shoulder. "Fucked if I know. There's no way any sane person might be able to conceive what is going on in that head of yours. You're what they call an unknown quantity, or better still, a loose cannon, which is why anyone in their right mind would steer clear of you."

"I don't need scum like you around me. You suck the life out of people with your evil ways."

"Do I fuck? You know nothing, man. You have no idea how to build a genuine relationship with folk. You're lost and vulnerable most of the time."

Owen raised an eyebrow. "You reckon. Well, let's have this out once and for all."

Lipsey raised a hand as Owen took a step forward. "Now wait just a minute. I'm not one for confrontation, only out on the battlefield, you know that as well as I do."

"Bollocks, not even then. You spent your whole career running, hiding behind others when the enemy was within range. Why was I the only one to see that?"

"You're making this up as you go along. Deluded, that's what you are. I've killed plenty of our adversaries over the years. It's not my fault you weren't around to witness the slaughters."

"There you go again, living in a dream world. It's what you've done since the day I first laid eyes on you. I recognised the type of man you were the instant I stood alongside you in the barracks. A mummy's boy like no other I had come across. But instead of being hounded by the bullies in the regiment, you took your cue and fooled the others into believing that you were a man not to be messed with. I witnessed the change in you, ribbed you about it in the beginning and, as your confidence grew in front of the others, you took your insecurities out on me. I should have walked the other way instead of climbing that mountain, let the Taliban rebel behead you. Isn't that how they usually kill infidels?"

"Screw you, Silver. Like I said, you've always been a weirdo. I wanted nothing to do with you in the army, but you kept lingering, a few feet from me at every turn. The others could see you were like a bloody limpet, clinging on to my every word. I hated every second you came near me. You made me cringe, you still do, while I'm standing here looking at you."

Owen was at the end of his tether. He withdrew the knife from his sleeve and pointed the blade at Lipsey who appeared to be mesmerised by the weapon.

"Don't do anything you're likely to regret, Owen." Lipsey's voice quivered.

"Don't worry, I won't. I'm going to enjoy every second of slicing the wickedness from your bones."

Lipsey glanced over his shoulder and made a run for it. Owen sprinted after him. Lipsey's longer legs had the advantage, and Owen was forced to up his game to keep up with the man slipping out of his grasp. Then an idea struck.

"Run, I'll just turn back and go to your house. Sixty-five Windsor Avenue, right? I'll knock on the door, introduce myself as an old army friend, and your wife, Justine, is bound to take pity on me and ask me in. Now, will your kids, Monty and Gemma, still be up at this time of night? Or will I take my knife and slit their throats while they sleep? Which do you think they'll prefer?"

Lipsey's pace faltered, and he spun around to face him. Owen caught up with him and came to a standstill barely two feet away from his angry opponent.

"Do what you have to do, but fucking keep my family out of it."

Owen ran his finger down the jagged edge of the blade and smirked. "I thought you would see sense, eventually. First, I have a few more reminders for you to take to your grave. Number one was the time we were in the Land Rover and the car in front hit an IED. We all jumped out to assist the injured men hit by the explosion, and you froze when the Taliban ambushed us. It was me who dragged you to safety and stuck a gun in your hand. You were a quivering wreck." He laughed. "And you pissed yourself."

"I did not. Not then, that came later. We were under fire for hours. Why mock me for that? That's cruel and heartless."

"But true, nonetheless. I'm merely pointing out your failings as a human being. Again, when the rest of the regiment showed up to rescue us, you strutted around, mimicking some kind of sodding superhero. And all the time you were cowering beside me, out of view of the others, but I witnessed it all. Your lack of class, your crumbling backbone in the face of adversity. All an utter joke, and you always had the front to brush it off and stick to your regime of jabbing the knife in my back at every opportunity. I want to know why before I slice you up into a gazillion pieces."

"It's all in your head, I was never like that. Army life plays havoc with your mind, it's doing that with yours right now."

"Fuck off. Have the courage of your convictions and tell me the truth for once in your life." Owen took a step closer.

Lipsey glared at him. "All right then, you want to know the truth?"

"It would make a change."

"I'll tell you. I was envious of you."

131

Owen shook his head in disbelief. "What the fuck are you talking about?"

"You had it all. You were strong where I was weak. I thought if I showed you up in front of the other men it would make me more popular in their eyes."

"For fuck's sake, and you have the audacity to call me a weirdo when you come out with bullshit like that."

Lipsey's head sank. "Do it. Don't hang around. I deserve what you have in store for me after the way I treated you. Once I started on that slippery slope and saw how the other men reacted to both of us, there was no turning back. I'll tell you this, though, I admired your courage and ability to push aside the hatred you must have had for me. That took guts. Many men would have given up at the first base, but not you."

Owen stalled, Lipsey's words of praise hitting him hard emotionally until he recalled yet another incident where the man had shown a blatant disregard for him as a human being. "Then there was the occasion when we were travelling down the river, dozens of crocodiles watching us from the banks, and you lost your balance and fell in. Three crocs immediately swam towards you. You screamed and splashed around, and the others in the boat scrabbled to the edge to try to haul you back in, however, you were so fixated on the approaching crocodiles that you forgot how to use your limbs. Rather than see you ripped to shreds before our eyes, I plunged into the river beside you, slipped below the water and shoved your arse over the side of the boat."

"I have nightmares about that one. My wife often has to wake me up, the sweat dripping off me." Lipsey shuddered and held his arms out to the sides. "All I can do is apologise again for putting you through all of that unnecessary shit."

"It's far too late for that. Anyway, like I believe you. Words are cheap, and it is actions that count in this life.

You've caused me problems throughout my service in the army, and now it's payback time." Pushing his sympathy gene aside, he took another step forward, and before Lipsey had the chance to talk him around a second time, he jabbed the knife into the bastard's gut. The manoeuvre came as a shock to both of them.

Lipsey's mouth gaped open, and he stared at the wound, shook his head and whispered, "I can't believe you did that. I didn't think you'd have it in you to attack me."

"What? You thought all this stalking you for weeks, if not months, taking note of your routine, wouldn't come to anything? You're going to be the third one I've killed this week."

"What? Why? Who were the others?"

"You're still asking too many questions. Take your punishment like a man. On the other hand, if you'd prefer to put up a fight, the end will come much sooner. The choice is yours."

"I'll go down fighting, you arsehole. Promise me one thing."

"Shoot!"

"If you finish me off, you'll leave my family alone."

"Yep, you have my word. And my word is my bond, it means something. Now, let's get this over and done with."

Lipsey nodded and swooped down to remove something from his ankle. He stood tall again with a flick knife in his right hand. "I'm going down fighting, I hope you're prepared for this, fucker." He sliced the air and got to within a few inches of Owen's midriff.

Owen caught Lipsey napping with his next strike when the serrated blade pierced his side. It scraped his rib bones, and Lipsey cried out and dropped the flick knife and slapped a hand over the wound.

"Caught you nicely there, didn't I?"

"You bastard. I didn't think you had the guts to do…"

"Now you know differently, don't you? It's okay, I'll finish you off quickly."

"Do it! Get it over with." Lipsey dropped onto his knees and swayed.

Owen did as requested. The blows came hard and fast, one swift movement after the other with no pausing to contemplate what he was doing in between. Eventually, Owen surfaced from his transfixed state and stared down at his nemesis who had, as expected, failed to match his survival instinct.

With a final cut to the man's throat, Owen left Lipsey lying on the path, in a pool of blood, and retraced his steps back to the Range Rover. Full of enthusiasm for life, his steps were light and energetic.

CHAPTER 7

"*W*hat do you want to see next?" Mark asked, his arm lovingly draped around her shoulders.

Before Sara could answer, her mobile rang. She glanced down at the screen, expecting it to be her father, and groaned. "Shit! I'd better get this, it's work. It might be important."

"Go for it. Want a top-up?" Mark got to his feet and picked up their glasses.

"Not for me, thanks." He left the room.

Sara answered the call. "Hello, DI Ramsey. What's up?"

"Sorry to trouble you at home, ma'am. It's the control centre here. I've been asked to contact you specifically. It's regarding an incident which occurred this evening."

"Where is it? What sort of incident?"

"Suspicious death down at the Grandstand Community Park. Do you know it?"

"I do. I take it the pathologist is at the scene and instructed you to get hold of me."

"She is, ma'am. Shall I call her back and tell her you'll be attending?"

"Yes, do that. Afterwards, can you contact my partner, DS Carla Jameson, see if she can also attend the crime scene?"

"I'll do it straight away, ma'am. Again, apologies for interrupting your evening."

"There's no need. I'm leaving now."

Mark entered the room and stared down at her. "By your expression, it's a bad one that needs your immediate attention."

"You're not wrong. Sorry, love. Lorraine is at the scene and asked for me specifically. I can only assume she believes the case is related to our ongoing investigation. Although, I won't know that for sure until I get there."

"No need to explain. It's your job, Sara. Go with my blessing, but only if you promise me you'll take care out there."

She rose from her seat and kissed him on the lips, tasting the remnants of the wine they were in the process of devouring. "Hopefully, the glass of wine I've consumed won't affect either my driving ability or my capabilities at the scene."

"It shouldn't do, not unless you're overly tired."

"I'm not. Shall I give you a call later?"

"I'll be disappointed if you don't. I'll stay up until elevenish. If you can't call, send me a text letting me know you're okay."

"I will." She hugged him and then flew into the hallway to slip on her shoes and coat. Misty followed her and wound her lithe body around Sara's legs. Sara swooped down and snuggled into her cat's fur. "Sorry to you, too. We were enjoying our cuddle, weren't we, little one?"

Misty rubbed her head on either side of Sara's chin. Mark came into the hallway and gently eased Misty out of her arms.

"She's a dab hand at making me feel guilty."

"Cats have a way of doing that. Stay safe, Sara." He leaned in for another kiss.

Sara collected her handbag and shot out of the door and into the car. A final wave goodbye after she reversed, and then she was on her way. Halfway through the trip into the city, Sara rang Carla. "It's me. How far away are you?"

"I'm five minutes out. You?"

"Around ten. I'll put my foot down and be with you short-ly." Sara avoided using her siren because there wasn't much traffic on the road. She managed to keep within the speed limit all the way to the location. When she arrived, she found two SOCO vans and the pathology van in the small car park, plus Carla's vehicle parked at the back, closest to the road. Her partner came over to join her. Sara switched off the engine and went to the boot to retrieve two paper protective suits. She handed one to Carla while she scanned the area. "Where are they all?"

"I'm presuming they must be inside the park."

With that, a tech in a white suit approached one of the vehicles. Sara flashed her warrant card. "DI Sara Ramsey. We've been summoned by Lorraine. Where is the victim?"

"I'll show you, but first, I need to get more evidence bags from the van. It's quite a trek."

"Is it bad?" Carla asked.

"Bad enough. Two ticks." He withdrew some clear plastic bags from the rear of the van and locked it up again.

The three of them set off into the park. Sara glanced ahead and could see the area where the others were working lit up by the temporary floodlights. The time was nine forty-five, and the area was quiet, apart from the investigation team.

A cordon had been set up. To the rear of it, a small crowd had gathered.

"Rubberneckers at two o'clock," Sara whispered.

137

"Yep, already noted. What is wrong with people?"

"Might be worth taking a pic or two on your phone, just in case."

"In case the killer is lingering, getting off on all the excitement?" Carla clarified.

"Yep. Stranger things have happened."

Carla removed her phone from her pocket and snapped off a few photos of the inquisitive crowd, most of whom were straining their necks to observe any gruesome details on display.

"Ah, ladies. Good of you to join me. Thought you'd be interested in this one this evening." Lorraine smiled and gestured for them to come closer.

Sara completed the Crime Scene Log then she and Carla ducked under the tape to step nearer to the bloody corpse lying at Lorraine's feet.

Sara took one look at the deceased, and her stomach clenched tightly into a large knot. "Bugger, this is bad."

Carla gulped beside her and turned away from the victim.

"Are you all right?" Sara asked.

"I will be once my meatballs and spaghetti sauce decide to go back down again."

"Bummer, try not to think about it."

"Not that easy to accomplish, no matter how hard I'm trying. I might need to step away for a few minutes, if that's all right."

"Go for it. Take your time. I have a feeling we're going to be stuck here for a while yet."

"Thanks. Not what I wanted to hear. I'll be back soon."

Sara took a step forward to stand alongside Lorraine. She was about to ask her pathologist friend her first question, but Carla vomiting behind her into a bag momentarily distracted her. "Ouch, poor Carla. If only the general public realised the amount of punishment our bodies take on cases such as this."

"My stomach is stronger than the largest diamond," Lorraine said with a broad grin.

"Lucky you. I had to fight hard to hang on to my evening meal. Hush now, I'm trying not to think about it. Have you had time to assess the body?"

"Yep, kind of. You know me, I don't like to confirm anything major until after the PM."

"I know. Humour me. Tell me what you do have."

"A man in his early thirties. ID in the bag over there says he's a serving soldier, Andrew Lipsey. There's also a picture of him with a woman and two young children around five and seven—might not be that accurate, I'm no expert on kids' ages. That's by the by, anyhoo. From what I can tell, he has several deep wounds in his torso, and the largest wound is in the throat."

"Is that the one which killed him?"

"I'm presuming that to be the case. Saying that, it could have been made immediately after his death with the amount of blood on show. There's a man waiting to answer all your questions over to the right, the older man with a bulldog lying beside him."

"I'll have a chat in a mo. What about any evidence we can latch on to?"

Lorraine gestured to a marker on the ground. "We found a flick knife. I'm in two minds as to whether it caused these injuries or not." She knelt beside the corpse and with gloved hands pulled back the victim's clothes to reveal a wound where the skin appeared to be torn. "At first glance, I thought this one looked as though it had been made with a serrated edge."

"Serrated edge?" Sara queried, her mind racing, searching for possible implements the killer might have used. "Any suggestions? I'm struggling to think of anything."

"My father used to go hunting with a serrated knife. I'm

not saying that's the case here, I'll need to do some research when I get back."

"Crap. I think I know the type you mean. Not pleasant. How many wounds are there?"

"Too many to count at the moment, and his clothes might be hiding a fair few. Over ten, I'd say, at a rough guesstimate."

"Intentional? Are we linking his death to the others? Torture involved, is that what we're seeing here?"

"Yes would be my response to all three questions, but don't quote me on that."

Carla rejoined them. "Sorry about that," she said in a raspy voice.

"Better?" Sara asked.

"I wouldn't go as far as to say that. Why the fuck does something that slips down so nicely come back up with a vengeance and burn like hell?"

"Do you have to go into detail?" Sara heaved.

"Sorry. I've got water in the car, but that's miles away."

"Hardly," Sara replied. "Go fetch it if you need to. Just stop whining."

"Charming. I'll keep my gob shut then, from now on." Carla folded her arms and tapped her foot.

Sara rolled her eyes at Lorraine.

"Carla, there's a bottle of water in my bag, help yourself," Lorraine said.

Carla walked over to the bag and sunk her hand in. She extracted the bottle and made a sound. "Eww... it's been used."

It was Lorraine's turn to roll her eyes at Sara. "Thems the breaks, hon. Take it or leave it, it makes no odds to me."

"I'll suffer, thanks."

"In silence, I hope," Sara was quick to add.

Carla said something indecipherable and shuffled her feet.

"Do you think the attack was prolonged?" Sara asked. "Wait, if there's another weapon here not associated with the victim's injuries, are we to assume he put up a fight?"

Lorraine raised her finger and said, "I wondered when that would sink in."

"I apologise for being slow, blame the distraction I've been dealing with."

Carla sighed beside her and muttered, "There's no need to rub it in."

Sara gently dug her in the ribs. "Stop being so sensitive, I'm only messing with you."

"I've just spewed my guts up. I'm hardly in the mood to have the piss taken out of me. So pardon me for breathing."

"Can we get back to work, ladies?" Lorraine interrupted their spat. "You asked if the attack was a prolonged one. I would be inclined to think it was. Whether we can class it as being torture like the previous two victims, that's where the doubts set in."

"Maybe the victim pulled the knife to protect himself and that altered the killer's strategy," Sara said after thinking the situation over for a few seconds. "Why here, out in the open? The others were killed later at night in an alley and a disused house, why the change?"

"Not much of a change from the alley to a park," Carla noted.

"Hmm… okay. But at this time of night when there are still people walking around? It's as though he wanted the victim to be found quickly, why?"

"Possibly, I'll give you that one," Lorraine replied. "Why don't you let us get on here and you can go and have a chat with the man who found him? Maybe he'll be able to fill in a few missing details for you."

"Did you get his name?" Sara asked, her gaze drifting over to the man chatting to the rubberneckers close to the cordon.

"I didn't, sorry."

"Come on, Carla, get your notebook out."

They crossed the damp grass to speak with the man. He took a few paces away from the crowd and smiled at them.

Sara flashed her warrant card and made the introductions. "I'm told you found the body Mr...?"

"It's Barlow, Frank Barlow. Yes, that's correct. He was alive when I got here but faded fast."

Sara faced Carla and raised an eyebrow. She returned her attention to the man and asked, "Did the victim say anything?"

"It was hard to hear him, what with that gash in his throat. I've never seen anything like this before and I never want to again, either."

"Can you tell us what he said?"

"I only caught a part of it. To me it sounded like river, slither, dither, could have been any of those. I got down on my knees." He pointed to the stains on his trousers. "To get closer to his mouth so I could hear but, by then, he was gone. I rang nine-nine-nine and told them he was dead. The ambulance showed up, but they left when this mob arrived. Is that the correct procedure? I thought the ambulance would take the body back to the hospital, but then, what do I bloody know?"

"Yes, that's correct. If they believe the victim has suffered a suspicious death. This is a crime scene now. You're going to have to recap where you went and if you touched the body so that we can eliminate any of your DNA, sir."

"Oh shit, I never thought about that. I shouldn't have gone near him, should I? But there again, what was I supposed to do, let him die without doing my very best to save his life?"

"It's a difficult one. You haven't done anything wrong, we merely need to get the facts from you."

"I felt his neck for a pulse, and it was very weak when I arrived. As soon as I touched his neck, his eyes shot open and scared the living daylights out of me. That's when he tried to speak and I got down on my knees. I don't suppose you know the best way to get the blood out of my trousers, do you? The wife is going to be livid. They're relatively new, she only bought them for me last Christmas."

"I'm sure a quick search on the internet will bring up various solutions for you, Mr Barlow."

"Thanks. I can't be doing with spending time on the internet, better things to do with my life than sitting at a computer all day long."

Ignoring his venting, Sara pressed on for more answers. "Did you happen to see anyone in the park either before or after you found the victim?"

"You know what? Now you mention it, yes, I did. A chap rushed past me. I had trouble making out if he was young or old, I'm presuming the former because he was wearing one of them hoodie-type jumpers. He had it pulled forward so I couldn't make out his features. I said good evening to him, he grunted and upped his pace. A few minutes later, Tilly and I walked around the corner and saw the man lying on the ground. Damn, do you think that was the killer?" He ran his hand over his balding head.

"Maybe. Which direction did he head in?"

"That way, towards B&Q. He was on foot, and I have no way of knowing if he had a vehicle waiting for him or not. I'm no bloody good, am I? Hopeless shit my wife always calls me. I've never been one to stick my nose where it wasn't wanted. Pisses her off good and proper most days, I can tell you."

"I'm sure. It takes a special person to take in what's going on around them twenty-four-seven, so I wouldn't be too hard on yourself."

"That'll be the missus, she'd have made a good copper with her nose for discreet facts and being downright nosey. I think she would have drawn the line at attending scenes like this, though, if I'm honest."

"Not everyone is capable of handling the blood and gore associated with our line of work." Sara cast a quick glance in Carla's direction, and her partner tutted.

"I couldn't," Mr Barlow said. "I know that. He must have suffered terribly before his death. I noticed there was a knife lying on the ground beside him. Do you think that was the murder weapon?"

"Possibly. We won't know until we obtain the post-mortem results."

"Ah, I see. What else do you need to know from me?"

"Anything else you're willing to share with us."

"I'm trying to think if there was anything but, no, that was all. Can I go now? If there's nothing more I can add, only Tilly needs her dinner. She'll start whining and causing a fuss soon."

"Yes, we'll make a note of your address and send a uniformed officer around to take a statement from you in the next day or so, if that's okay?"

"Only too happy to help, as long as it doesn't bring trouble to my door."

"It won't, I'm sure of it." Sara tried to reassure the man, although sometimes she doubted if it was true, judging by past experience.

After he gave Carla the address, Sara bid Mr Barlow farewell, and she and Carla returned to the crime scene. They put their shoe covers on and sidled up next to Lorraine.

"Do you need us to stick around or can we get off now?" Sara asked.

"Part-timers."

"Hardly, we have a family's life we need to ruin before we can call it a day."

"I was jesting. I don't envy you. A couple of things before you go. We have a footprint of interest and we'll be dusting the knife for prints in case the killer touched it at all."

"That's a positive note to end on, thanks. I'll be in touch later."

"We'll be here for a while. I might leave the PM until the morning, but there again, I might not. I'll see what frame of mind I'm in later. It's been a long day already."

"No rush, he's not going anywhere, although the sooner we have the results the better from my point of view. However, the last thing I'd want to do is to put you under pressure."

"You won't. If anything, I always put myself under pressure. That's why I have no fucking social life."

Sara smiled, not wanting to get into the same old argument they'd had for the past five years or more about Lorraine finding someone interesting to settle down with. Sara and Carla had done their very best to matchmake for her over the past few months, and it had proven disappointing on all fronts. "Do what you need to do, Lorraine TTFN."

She and Carla removed their protective suits and booties and placed them in the evidence bag then returned to their vehicles. "I'll follow you," Sara said, aware that Carla was far more knowledgeable about the area.

"It's not too far. We should be there in five minutes."

"Okay. This is going to be a tough one. I'll try and rehearse what needs to be said en route." Sara slipped behind the steering wheel and waited for Carla to sort herself out and drive off. No officer liked this part of the job, especially when the victim had left a young family behind.

. . .

CARLA DREW up outside an end-of-terrace in a block of what looked like council houses. A small green lay at the front of the properties, cutting off the private road accessing the houses from the main road. Sara thought it was a good idea for the occupants with young children to keep safe. She left the vehicle and met up with Carla at the gate.

"Are you ready for this?" Carla asked.

"Nope, are you?"

"You're going to be the one doing all the work, I'm just here for moral support and to take notes."

Sara tutted and looked up at the lights on in the bedroom upstairs. A woman was peering out of the window at them. "We've been spotted. Now I don't know whether to ring the bell or not."

"I'd leave it for a second or two, see if she appears."

Moments later, as if the woman had overheard their conversation, she left the window and within seconds the front door opened. "Hello, did you want something? My kids are asleep, thank you for not ringing the bell."

"We thought as much. Sorry to trouble you, Mrs Lipsey. I'm DI Sara Ramsey, and this is my partner, DS Carla Jameson. Would it be possible to come in and speak with you about an urgent matter?"

Her hand covered her chest. She shook her head and gasped. "This is about Andy, isn't it? He was due home about an hour ago, and I've been unable to contact him via his phone."

"Inside would be better," Sara urged gently.

She stepped aside, and they entered the property. "Would you prefer it if we removed our shoes?"

"I don't care. What's going on? Please tell me." She gestured for them to go in the front room, and they all took a seat before Sara answered.

"I'm sorry, there's no easy way of breaking the news to

you. This evening, the body of a person we believe to be your husband was found in the Grandstand Community Park."

Tears brimmed, and she shook her head from side to side. "No, this can't be true. Not Andy, it couldn't have been."

"I'm sorry, we'll need a formal identification to be sure, but according to the ID we found on him at the scene, it confirms it's him." Sara surveyed the room, and her gaze halted on a photo of the couple. In her opinion, there was no mistaking they had the right person.

"But he couldn't have died, he only went to the gym."

"Which gym, can you tell me that?"

"Perfect Pecs, I believe it's called." She removed a tissue from her cardigan pocket and wiped her eyes. "Oh shit, what the hell am I going to tell the kids?"

"Is there someone you'd like us to call to come and sit with you?"

"My mother. She lives the closest."

"Do you have her number?"

"I'll ring her." She picked up the phone that was lying on the arm of her chair and stared at it. "No wonder he didn't respond to my messages or calls." She angled the phone at Sara. "I've been ringing him for the past hour or so. He said he'd be back by nine at the latest."

"I'm sorry for your loss. It must be a shock to know he won't be coming home again."

"It is. Let me call my mum." She punched a number and stared at the wall ahead of her. "Sorry to ring so late, Mum. I need you to come over... yes, right away. No, the kids are all right, it's Andy, something has happened... okay, I'll see you soon. The police are here... don't stress, just get here." She replaced the phone on the chair and leaned her head back. "She's on her way. Panicking as usual. She won't be long. I feel bloody disorientated. He went off this evening in a good mood, and now, he's gone."

"What time did he set off to the gym?"

"Around sevenish, I was bathing the children at the time."

"Does he generally walk there?"

"When it's not tipping down with rain, he does. He walks the same route and takes the shortcut through the park. Is that where you found him? I can't remember what you told me, everything is such a daze."

"Yes, on the path in the park."

"How did he die? Was it through the exertion at the gym? He's in the army, you see. I keep telling him that he pushes his body too hard. Sorry, pushed himself. God, will I ever get used to talking in the past tense?"

"It will become second nature after a while. So you're telling me your husband was a fit man?"

"Yes, very fit. You haven't told me how he died."

"Unfortunately, your husband was involved in some kind of altercation with someone and he died as a result of the wounds he received."

"A *fight*? Is that what you're saying?"

"So it would appear. Do you know if your husband carried a knife?"

She closed her eyes and tilted her head back. "Yes, I warned him not to. Told him it would only lead to trouble, but he chastised me for being silly and told me not to worry as he could take care of himself. Do you know what the fight was about?"

"No, or who it was with. Your husband suffered severe injuries. He was found by someone walking their dog through the park. The man tried to comfort him. Your husband said one word before he passed away, but the witness couldn't quite make out what he was trying to say."

"Am I supposed to know what that means? I don't understand, either he spoke or he didn't, which is it?"

148

"He mentioned slither, river or dither. Do any of those mean anything to you?"

"No, I can't say they do. Maybe he was talking about the River Wye. He goes there quite a bit when he's not away with the army, you know, he likes to fish. Sometimes he'll take the kids with him to give me a break."

"Okay, we'll make a note of it. Has he had any cause for concern lately? Fallen out with anyone?"

"Not that I know of. He's away for months at a time."

"When was he due back on duty?"

"At the end of next week, hence visiting the gym. He said he was going to the gym every night until he goes away. His fitness levels meant a lot to him."

"And he went to the same gym all the time?"

"Yes, that's right."

"What about friends in the area, does he have many?"

She nodded. "He was fairly popular. Some from way back in school. I don't think he's hooked up with anyone new in the last few months, not to my knowledge."

Just then the front door opened and closed noisily, and a frantic-looking woman dressed in jeans and a bright-pink sweatshirt barged into the room. "What in God's name is going on, Justine?" She rushed over to her daughter's side, knelt beside her and grasped her hand.

"It's Andy, he's gone, Mum."

Her mother's gaze drifted between Sara, Carla and her daughter. "Gone where? What are you talking about, love?"

Justine sniffled. "He's dead."

Her mother fell back onto her haunches and stared at Sara, her mouth gaping open. "Wh... what?" she eventually asked.

"I'm sorry. Andy lost his life this evening on the way home from the gym," Sara confirmed.

"How? Dear Lord, I can't believe what I'm hearing."

149

"We suspect it was some kind of altercation."

"A fight? That's not like him. I know he can be a little hot-headed at times but he doesn't usually get into fights, does he, Justine?"

"No, that's true."

"Hot-headed?" Sara picked up on what she considered a significant fact that Justine, as yet, had failed to mention.

"Sorry, I should have said. He did have a slight temper."

"A temper that flared up willy-nilly? Or did he manage to contain it most of the time?" Sara watched with interest the look that shot between the mother and daughter. "It would be helpful if you didn't keep any details from us."

"It flared up now and again. He's not used to being around the kids as much as I am. Their shenanigans wear him down when it gets towards the end of his leave."

"That's why he goes to the gym, to vent his frustrations out on the equipment rather than the kids, is that it?"

Justine covered her eyes with her hand and whispered, "Yes."

"Forgive me for asking, Justine, but did Andy ever lash out at you?"

She swallowed and avoided looking her mother in the eye. "He's hit me a couple of times."

"What?" her mother shouted. "Why didn't you tell me? I would have wiped the bloody floor with him. How dare he lay a hand on you?" She gasped. "What about the kids? Did he ever strike them?"

"No. I warned him that if he ever laid a hand on them, he'd end up in hospital. I handled the situation, Mum, there was no need to involve you in my marriage dispute."

"Well, pardon me for caring what happens to you, child. If your father was alive today…"

"He's not, though, is he? And now my husband is dead, too."

Her mother reached forward and hugged her. They both ended up crying. Sara's heart twitched at the touching scene. The two women would be relying on each other for the foreseeable future.

"Sorry to intrude on your grief," Sara said, "but I only have a few questions left, if you don't mind?"

"Heartless," Justine's mother said.

"Hush, Mum. They're only doing their job. We want the person who robbed us of Andy caught, don't we?"

"I suppose so. Go on then, ask your questions."

Sara cleared her throat. "I'd like to ask you if Andy possibly knew a Ben Connor or a Ned Frost."

Justine's forehead pinched into a frown. "I don't think so. At least, I don't recognise the names. But you'll have to forgive me, my mind is very fuzzy and not functioning right."

"I understand. If I leave you my card and you remember the names, will you give me a call?"

"What's so special about the men you mentioned?" her mother asked.

"They're part of the investigation. These two men have also lost their lives this week, leading me to believe there might be a possible connection linking all three cases."

"Three murders? And all the men were targeted by the same killer?" Justine asked, shaking her head.

"So it would seem. Although we have nothing concrete to signify that as yet."

"Then why say it?" Justine's mother snapped back.

"You're right. I shouldn't have mentioned it. Forgive me. Is there anything else you think we should know?"

"With regards to what?" Justine asked.

"Anything that you believe might help with our enquiries."

"No, I don't think so. What happens now? Do I get to see him?"

"The pathologist will be carrying out a post-mortem in the next day or two, and then she will invite you to formally identify his body."

"Oh God, I'm not sure if I'll be able to do that."

"Hush now, you will because I will be right there beside you," her mother said. She patted Justine's hand.

"I know, but all the same... I'm at a loss what to tell the kids. Should I tell them right away or leave it a few days? They're bound to ask where he is. He was due to take them to the cinema tomorrow to see the latest Disney film."

"Don't worry, we'll put our heads together and come up with a reasonable excuse. You'll know when the time is right to tell them he's never coming home again."

Sara rose from her seat. "We're going to leave you to it unless you have any further questions you'd like to ask."

"I can't think of any, not right now. I want to thank you for coming and for being so patient with me. The news came out of the blue. I'm not sure if I reacted as you expected to or not. I apologise if I didn't."

Sara smiled. "In my experience, people react in different ways when dealing with grief. I apologise for being the bearer of such sad news. Here's my card. Ring me day or night if you need to chat."

Carla joined Sara at the door, and together they left the room.

Justine's mother entered the hallway. "I want you to bust a gut to find whoever did this. That girl in there didn't deserve this. I know I've never seen eye to eye with my son-in-law but I would never wish this upon him. Someone needs to pay. Is there a chance this person could come here, after my daughter and the kids?"

"I don't think so. I'll make arrangements for a constable to be on duty on the doorstep for the next twenty-four hours, if you think that would give Justine some peace of mind."

"It would, and me."

"I'll call the station before I set off. Thank you for coming to sit with her. We'll be in touch soon."

"You do that. We want to know the minute you have caught someone. I don't expect to see it all over the news before we've been told, got that?"

"Don't worry, you won't. Goodnight."

As soon as they stepped over the threshold, Sara felt the waft of the door being shut behind her. "Blimey, I'd hate to get on the wrong side of her. Maybe that's why Justine decided to keep the abuse a secret."

"Abuse? He hit her a couple of times," Carla retaliated.

Sara raised an eyebrow and led the way back to the cars. "Just for the record, one hit signifies abuse in my eyes. I'm shocked that you should think otherwise, considering what you went through with your ex."

"Don't start, Sara. I messed up, in more ways than one. Where to now?"

"I'm heading into the station. I have a few things I need to organise. You can either join me or go home."

"I'll join you, if that's all right with you?"

"Of course it is. We can thrash out the details of the cases after I've made the arrangements I need to make."

"Deal."

BACK AT THE STATION, Carla went on ahead while Sara stopped at the reception area to have a chat with the night desk sergeant. He assured her that he would send a constable over to Justine Lipsey's house within the hour.

Sara trudged up the stairs on weary legs; the tiredness

153

had hit her in the car on the way. There was only one thing that would help to overcome her weariness—a caffeine fix.

Carla had already lined the drinks up and was standing next to the whiteboard with the marker pen in her hand. "I went ahead and made a start, I hope you don't mind?"

"Of course not. I owe you an apology for snapping at you back there."

"You don't, it was a foolish remark I made, your castigation was justified."

"Thanks for understanding. It still rattles my cage what that bastard did to you. He had no right to treat you the way he did. No man should ever lay a hand on a woman, fact."

"Stop! Stop going over old ground. He's out of my life for good. I'm happier than I've ever been with Des, thanks to your intervention."

"The pleasure was all mine. Right, I'm glad we've cleared the air. Hang on, before we get on, I think we should ring Mark and Des, make them aware of what we're up against."

"I actually rang Des from the car. I told him we'd be working through the night."

"Bugger, I hope it doesn't come to that. We'll see how things pan out. I'll just ring Mark." She nipped into her office, leaving her cup on the desk, with the intention of making her call a brief one. "Hey, you. It's me. Checking in as instructed."

"Thank goodness. Where are you?"

"I'm at the station with Carla. We're going to sit down and assess all the cases. It could be a late one, so don't wait up for me."

"I won't. Don't work too hard, Sara, you'll be no good to anyone if you don't get some rest."

"We're determined to find this bastard, Mark. If it takes us working long hours to do it then so be it. Sorry, I didn't mean to shout. This investigation is beginning to get to me. Three bodies in a week has left me reeling."

"I know. You care. I get that, all I'm advising is don't wear yourself out."

"I hear you and I promise."

"Take care, darling. I'll either see you later or speak to you in the morning, should you decide to stay there all night."

"Sleep well, Mark. Thanks for understanding."

"Always. Love you."

"I love you, too, now and forever."

She ended the call and drifted back into the incident room, her eyes misting up with unshed tears.

"Hey, what's wrong?" Carla asked.

"Ignore me. I'm overtired and overemotional. He never ceases to amaze me."

"Mark is a real gem. It's obvious how much he loves you and admires the work you do."

"Anyway, let's push through the exhaustion and go over the leads we have so far. What are we missing?"

"Nothing from what I can tell, but we must be, unless the killer is being super careful. I think he's slipped up tonight by what Lorraine said at the crime scene."

Sara held up her crossed fingers. "Here's hoping. Going back to the other cases... On the Ned Frost case, was there any news on the cars passing the car park at the time he left the pub?"

"I'm not sure. I'll make a note to chase that up in the morning."

"Okay. What other links have we got?"

"Tess being abused by Ben Connor and Andy Lipsey hitting his wife a few times, could that be a connection?"

"Maybe a loose one. Neither woman stated that she sought help for the abuse, so I think we'd be wise leaving that to one side at present."

"If you say so. I still think there might be a tenuous link."

"We'll park it for now but keep it in mind. What careers did all three victims have? Soldier, assistant manager in a sports shop and a carpenter. I can't for the life of me see any connections there."

Carla scratched the side of her head with the pen she was holding. "Nope, neither do I. What about their ages? Thirty, thirty and thirty-three. Could there be something in that?"

Sara raised a pointed finger. "You could be onto something. Maybe the men all went to the same school. Definitely worth delving into."

"Or perhaps they lived in the same area as kids. Or even hung out in the same gang."

Sara's nod gained momentum. "Both possibilities we should explore. We're on a roll."

"I wouldn't get too excited, not yet."

"Then we have the ex-boyfriend of Sophie to consider, the woman carrying on with Ben Connor. I'm not willing to dismiss his involvement at this stage."

"Hmm... if you say so. What about Tess? We had her in the frame at the beginning. Has that all changed now?"

"The jury is still out for me. What we need to do is start the searches going for Andrew Lipsey and then we'll be better armed for when the rest of the team come into work in the morning. Why don't we check through the social media posts together? We won't be able to access his bank account until the morning; we'll leave that in Christine's expert hands."

Carla stepped away and flicked the switch on her computer to bring it to life then logged in to Facebook and searched for first *Andrew Lipsey* and came up blank, then she typed in *Andy Lipsey*, and the victim's profile appeared on the screen. "Here we go."

"Let's go through all his posts this year. He posted a fair

bit from time to time, I suppose when he was off duty, so it might take us a while."

Carla scrolled through the numerous smutty jokes and dirty memes he preferred to post. These were intermingled with photos of family days out with the children. He and Justine seemed happy enough in most of the photos, and he appeared to enjoy his time playing with his two children from what Sara could tell. They visited fun parks and had gone on several days out with the children. Going back a couple of years, before the pandemic, they even went on a holiday to Greece.

"All appears good there. His friends list is about average, around the thousand mark. Maybe we should take a closer look at those, see if anyone stands out there."

It didn't. Not really. He wasn't friends with either Ben or Ned, according to his profile.

Sara sighed. "It's all very frustrating, and I'm not sure if all this is going to lead us anywhere. What else have we got?"

"We could take a look at Ned's and Ben's Facebook pages again, see if anything prods us there."

"Do it."

Unfortunately, the response was the same, nothing linking either of the men to Andy.

"I hate to say it but I believe we're floating down the river approaching the rapids without a paddle to save us. Why? What are we bloody missing, Carla?"

Her partner shrugged and sank back in her chair. "Pass. It's beyond me. We need something to come our way soon."

"Yep, I can read your mind: before the killer strikes again."

"I was too afraid to say it out loud."

CHAPTER 8

 *he next day*

OWEN STOPPED off at the gym, completed a mini workout, dived under the shower, and then changed into the new jeans and polo shirt he'd bought that afternoon. He was now back in the Range Rover on his way to Tess's house, hopeful for another chance encounter with the woman he loved.

He studied his eyes in the rear-view mirror, his lack of sleep from the previous night evident in the bloodshot sclera. *My God, I'm a sodding mess. She's gonna take one look at me and walk in the other direction. Still, it's the chance I'm willing to take.* He drove to the other side of town and parked thirty feet away from her house until she came home from work. *She can't be that grief-stricken if she's back at work already. So there's hope for me yet. Ben had deserved to die after laying a hand on her. He deserved it full stop. The bastard shouldn't have taken his frustrations out on her. She was far too good for him. Now he's out of the way, all I have to do is worm myself back into her life and make her feel like a princess again. Let her know how much she's loved and adored. All I've done this week has been for her. That's true love!*

Tess got off the bus and walked towards the house, carrying two heavy bags of shopping. If he'd been parked at the other end of the road, he could have unburdened her, that would have eased him into her good books again.

Owen took the chance and removed his phone from his pocket which he intended to use as a distraction. He set off on foot towards Tess's house on the other side of the road, so she didn't notice him. That was the plan anyway. Now that he was within a few feet of her house, he toyed with his mobile and sneakily took a peek up now and again. Tess had stopped to dig her key out of her handbag and was about to insert it in the lock. He had to make his move, it was now or never.

"Hey, Tess. I thought it was you. Fancy seeing you here. Is this where you live?"

Her expression was one of confusion. "What are you doing around these parts?"

"Ah, I dropped a friend off around the corner and thought I'd come this way to go to the gym, thought the walk would do me some good."

"Oh, I see. Do you always go to the gym armed only with your mobile?"

"Ah, yes, silly me. I knew I had forgotten something. I'd better nip back for my gym bag, it's in the car. Here, why don't I give you a hand with those? They look heavy."

"I'm fine. This is my home. You get off, it was nice seeing you again."

"You, too. It's becoming a habit, keep bumping into each other like this. Maybe it's the universe trying to tell us something."

"Like what?"

"That we're meant to be together."

Her eyes widened, and she shuffled on the spot then inserted the key in the lock. "Bah, you don't believe in all that rubbish, do you?"

"There has to be something in it. The great oracle, Noel Edmunds, is always going on about it."

"There you have it then. If he believes in all that tosh then it must be true. Excuse me, Owen. I really must be getting on."

"Umm… I was wondering if you'd like to go out for a drink sometime."

"I… umm… it's the wrong time for me, I'm sorry, but the answer has to be no."

"What? Why? I thought we were getting on great together."

She pushed the door open and picked up her bags, letting out a grunt at the weight pulling on her back.

He seized the opportunity and removed the bags from her hand. "I'll take them, they're far too heavy for a wee dot like you to carry." He barged past her into the hallway.

Tess remained glued to the spot outside the house. "Thanks, I can manage from there. You have to go now."

He grinned. "I've got time for a cuppa."

"Sorry, I haven't. I'm… oh yes, I'm expecting a group of friends any moment. You'd better go." She stepped to the side.

"Oh, that's disappointing. Anyone I might know?"

"I doubt it. My life has moved on considerably since… well, since we were together, Owen."

"I know, it has a tendency to do that, doesn't it?" He snorted.

Tess folded her arms. "I don't want to appear rude but I need to get on, so if you wouldn't mind leaving now."

He hopped over the threshold. "Sorry, I got carried away. Only trying to help you out, Tess. How about that drink? Can we make arrangements to meet up for another day?"

"I don't think that would be a good idea. Not at the moment."

"Oh, yes, I didn't mean right now. What about next week sometime? Or at the weekend even?"

Her mouth fixed into a straight line. He remembered the expression well from when they used to be partners; she was not best pleased with his suggestion.

"I've asked you to leave. Kindly do as I ask or I'll be forced to contact the police."

"You what? The police, why?"

"Because I believe you're harassing me."

He backed away and put his hands up in front of him. "Whoa, I'm doing no such thing. I helped you with your shopping and asked you out on a date, how is that harassing you?"

Her eyes narrowed, and her head tilted. "And it was pure coincidence that you happened to be walking down my road just as I was coming home from work?"

His hands flipped over, and his mouth twitched nervously. "It was. I can't believe you're saying this. We were getting on so well together."

"You're unbelievable, Owen Silver. I'm fucking grieving the loss of my boyfriend, and here you are, hounding me on my doorstep, begging for me to give you another chance. Have you truly forgotten how and why our relationship ended in the first place?"

"No, but that's in the past. I'm offering you the palm of friendship or whatever it's called, I forget now."

"I don't know what the right term is either and I don't care. All I want is for you to get out of my life. I can't cope

161

with this harassment. I'm in touch with a police officer at the moment because of the way Ben died. All I have to do is call her and she'd come over and arrest you. I'm sodding grieving, now leave me alone." Tess raced into the house and slammed the door in his face.

He stood there mortified, glancing up and down the road, embarrassment darting through him. He opened the letterbox and shouted, "I'm sorry. I was out of order, please forgive me, Tess. Open the door and let's sort this out. I didn't mean to upset you. I would never want to do that."

"Get lost, Owen. Don't ever come here again."

He slammed the letterbox shut, stood upright and reluctantly made his way back to the car. He kicked out at the front tyre and then dropped in behind the steering wheel. There, he punished it with his flying fists and picked up his notebook from the passenger seat. On the last page of the book was the name Ethan Tristram, his next victim. He flicked on the ignition to check the clock on the dashboard and compared it to the notes he'd made regarding Ethan's daily routine. He would be at the Rose and Crown by now, on an afternoon session.

Owen drove to the location and parked in a space opposite the pub, his conversation with Tess, if you could call it that, going round and round in his head like a revolving turntable. His anger rose with every extra minute he spent in the car, waiting.

Until finally, after nearly an hour of Owen sitting in a pressure pot, Ethan came out of the pub and walked off down the road, a slight teeter now and then, his legs failing to cooperate properly. Owen would bide his time and follow at a snail's pace until he was ready to pounce. He was aware of the direction Ethan would take in his quest to get home before his wife came back from work.

Not far. Another few feet and he'd make his move.

Now, I need to jump him now or it will be too late. Just then, a woman walking a terrier came around the corner, and the opportunity was lost. It was cutting it a bit fine, but another few feet wouldn't hurt, they couldn't.

Ethan turned the next corner, and Owen gunned the accelerator. The Rover came to a stop just ahead of Ethan. His old army pal abruptly halted and stared at him.

"What the fuck do you want, Silver?"

"You, arsehole. It's payback time."

Ethan's eyes formed tiny slits. "Let's face it, mate, you ain't got the bottle."

Owen marched towards him. The knife slipped from up his sleeve into his palm and nestled into his clenched fist. "We'll see about that, shall we?"

"Bollocks. You might talk a good game, but I know you won't walk the walk, fucker. You're clueless where combat is concerned. I've spent enough years in the army clearing up your mistakes to know that."

Without detecting any hint of a slur, Owen wondered if he'd misjudged Ethan. Was he about to go into battle with someone stronger and more adept than him? There was only one way to find out. He flipped the knife between his two hands, his aim to confuse his opponent.

Ethan laughed at his antics. "You always were a bullshitter, weren't you, knobhead?"

Owen caught the knife in his right hand and jabbed, but Ethan reacted swiftly and took a step back, out of reach. Owen's temper flared. He jabbed a couple more times and eventually nicked Ethan's stomach.

"What the fuck is wrong with you? What's the object of trying to take me down after all these years?"

"I repeat, it's payback time. I've been building up to this. Seeking revenge on those who have wronged me in the past."

"Hey, I bet that list is super long, mate, because everyone

in the battalion hated you. We all cheered and downed a few drinks the night we heard you got kicked out of the army."

"Fuck off. I know you all hated me, it was frigging obvious from day one, but I stuck with it, did my best to become one of the crowd, to win you over."

"But it didn't work, did it?" Ethan mocked him in a girly voice.

Owen ran at him, the knife pointed at Ethan's chest, but he dodged to the side and turned to face him again with his hands raised at an angle. It was then that Owen remembered his opponent winning awards for his karate endeavours.

Fuck, I've screwed up. I should have tackled him from behind, caught him unaware. Furious, he ran at him again and added a growl into the mix.

Ethan stepped to the side and clouted him on the back of the head. Owen tumbled to the ground but regained his composure and bounced back onto his feet.

"Keep your filthy hands off me, shithead."

"If you say so. Come on, Silver, give it your best shot. I'm giving you permission to come at me again, if you've got the balls."

Owen paused for an instant, doubt entering his mind whether he had the cojones to continue with the attack or not. Seconds later, he charged again. This time, the knife sliced back and forth as he ran.

Ethan grunted and stumbled before he dropped to one knee. Hearing a noise behind him, Owen peered over his shoulder to find a man in his thirties standing there.

"What the fuck is going on? Oi you, drop your weapon. I'm an off-duty police officer."

Fuck, fuck, fuck! Owen bolted and jumped into the car. He didn't care if the copper took down his numberplate or not, he could easily nick another car later.

He kept a watchful eye on proceedings behind him. The copper was on the phone while checking Ethan was okay at the same time. No doubt calling for backup.

"Shit. I need to dump this vehicle quickly before they catch up with me."

CHAPTER 9

*A*t four p.m., weariness had descended, and Sara found herself pushing through the barrier to get her over the finishing line for the day. She had been at the station all night, and although she had slept at her desk from three until five, it would never make up for not getting her usual eight hours in the comfort of her own bed. She had insisted Carla went home at two. Her partner hadn't argued and had agreed to come into work early to help out and had shown up at seven that morning.

Sara was taking a five-minute break in her office. The phone interrupted her resting her eyes. "Sorry to trouble you, ma'am, thought you might want to hear about this right away."

"What's that, Jeff?"

"There's been an incident. A man wielding a knife on a serving soldier. One of our off-duty lads confronted the thug, and he drove off in a black Range Rover."

"Interesting. Was anyone injured?"

"Yes, the soldier took a knife in the side a couple of times. By all accounts, he put up a good fight. He's on his way to the hospital now, thought you might want to have a chat with him."

"On my way now, Jeff, thanks for the heads-up."

Sara ended the call, stretched the knots out of her back, circled her shoulders a few times and left the office. "Carla, we need to get to the hospital. Another soldier has been attacked. One of our lot interrupted the assault on the man, and he's been whisked off to hospital. A black Range Rover was involved. Get me a list of all those in the area, Craig. Let's find this bastard."

"Umm... can I add that there was a black Rover caught on CCTV passing the pub as Ned Frost left the other night?" Barry called across the room.

"Dig into that for me, Barry. Get a plate number. I'll have a word with the desk sergeant, see if his guy at the scene caught the details of the one involved. Let's hope we're onto something here."

"Fingers crossed," Carla said, "We could bloody do with a break."

"You're not wrong. Are you fit?" Sara asked, slipping into her jacket.

"I wouldn't go that far after working half the night, but I'm eager to get on the road."

"Let's go!"

AT THE HOSPITAL, Sara parked in the closest space she could find, and they tore through the main entrance, stopping at the reception desk to see if the victim had been admitted.

"His name?"

Sara chewed her lip and apologised. "Sorry, I didn't get it. It would come up as a knife wound, if that helps."

The redheaded receptionist tutted and then smiled.

"You're in luck. A man came in about forty minutes ago. Go through to A&E, ask down there for Ethan Tristram."

"You're a star. I'll be sure to remember you at Christmas."

"Whatever," the receptionist called after her.

They trotted down the long winding corridor, following the coloured strip for the Accident and Emergency Department. Fortunately, adrenaline pumped through Sara's weary body, reviving it en route.

In the reception area, Sara spotted the off-duty police officer. "Over there. I can't remember his name but I recognise his face."

"I think it's Colin Rogers. Don't quote me on that one, though."

The officer recognised them and came towards them. "Hi, PC Colin Rogers, ma'am. It's good of you to come down here."

"Thanks for jumping in while off-duty. What condition is he in?"

"He was sitting up talking to me in the back of the ambulance. I've got a name for you."

"Of the attacker?"

"Yes. He told me he was a former soldier who got discharged with PTSD. His name is Owen Silver."

"Carla, feed that information back to the team, see what they can find out about him."

Carla nodded and took a few paces back to make the call.

"How bad is he? Will he survive?" Sara asked, her gaze flicking around the waiting area.

"I'm no expert, but they seemed like superficial wounds to me. They're cleaning him up a bit and then sending him for X-rays."

"I'm going to ask if I can see him. Wait here."

Sara called after a nurse darting from one cubicle to another.

She poked her head around the curtain. "Can we have a bit of hush in this area, if you don't mind?"

"Sorry." Sara flashed her ID. "Urgent matter. I'd like to speak with Ethan Tristram, if possible?"

"I'll have to check with the doctor. I'll be right back." She deposited the jug of water on the table next to a woman in her fifties and told the patient she wouldn't be long. Then she jogged along the corridor and went through the swing doors. She appeared moments later with a doctor wearing a blue uniform.

"This is Doctor Kingsley. He can answer all your questions." The nurse returned to tend to the patient she was seeing to before Sara interrupted her.

Carla joined them.

"Hello, Doctor, how is he?"

"We'll be sending him down for an X-ray, checking for any internal injuries before we stitch him up. I believe he had a lucky escape as no main arteries or any of the major organs were affected."

"Good to hear. Is it possible to have a quick chat before he goes down?"

"The briefest of chats, yes, that would be possible. I know he's eager to speak with you. Come this way."

"Everything all right?" Sara asked Carla on the way.

"Yep, they're digging deep on Silver now. Hopefully, we'll be better informed when we get back to the station."

The doctor asked them to put on protective aprons and masks while in triage and showed them to Ethan's bedside. Sara introduced them. The man's cheeks were pale. He moved, winced and clutched his side.

"Good to see you. Can we make this quick?" he asked.

"Of course. If they come to collect you, we'll pause the interview. Can you tell us what happened?"

"Yeah, the guy you want is Owen Silver. He was in my

169

regiment, 266 Battery. We're based in Bristol. He was a right wanker when he was signed up. He got discharged a few years ago because of PTSD."

"Why did he come after you?"

"He said it was revenge. I didn't like going into battle beside him, he was a loose cannon. I wasn't the only one who felt that way, no one was keen on fighting alongside him."

"Why?"

"He was unreliable and unpredictable at times. A proper Jekyll and Hyde character. You never knew how to take him, whether he was having a laugh or being serious. Always had that same stupid look on his face."

"Hard to read emotionally?"

"That's it, you've got it spot on."

"Did he say anything else?"

"Not really. I got the sense he was stalking me. I'd not long left the pub and was walking home. Maybe he thought I was drunk and that's why he chose to attack. I wasn't, though, I don't drink much during the day, only go down there to be sociable. I'm on leave. I enjoy a pint or two but no more than that during the day."

"How did he approach you?"

"He stopped ahead of me in that big fancy car of his and pulled out a knife. He'd clearly forgotten that I'm a martial arts expert. I gave as good as I got. Clobbered him and floored him at one point. It made him angrier. He came at me repeatedly. Then he started swinging the knife from side to side. He sliced me a couple of times, but I blocked out the pain. I wasn't about to give in to him. That doesn't mean to say I wasn't grateful for one of your lads showing up. It took the pressure off, given the injuries I was carrying. I got the impression he was about to kill me."

"More than likely. Do you know Ben Connor?"

His brow furrowed, and he shook his head.

"Ned Frost?"

"The name sounds familiar, but I'm not a hundred percent sure."

"What about Andrew Lipsey?"

He nodded and inclined his head. "Andy is in the same regiment as me. What about them?"

"All three men have been murdered this week."

"Shit! By Silver?"

"We're presuming that to be the case, yes. Given what's happened to the other men, I'd say you had a lucky escape today."

His hand slid through his hair and rested on top of his head. "Fuck, it sounds like it. You've got to catch him before he kills someone else. He told me he had a long list of people he needed to pay back."

"Did he mention any other names to you?"

"No. The man's a loon, proper crazy fucker. You need to nab him and lock him up."

"We're doing our best. It would be helpful if you could give us a clue where to find him. I take it he lives in the area?"

"I reckon he does. I don't know his address, if that's what you're after. Ask that copper who intervened, I think he took down the numberplate of the vehicle."

"He's still here, we've had a chat with him and we've already put out an alert on the Rover. It would be great if you could tell us what you know about him."

"Not a lot apart from what I've told you already. Hang on, I seem to remember he had a girlfriend, don't ask me her name, it was a while ago, something beginning with T, I think it was."

"Tania? Teresa? Tina?" Sara asked.

"Tess?" Carla threw in."

He clicked his thumb and forefinger and pointed at Carla.

"That's the one. Tess, like Tess Daly off that dancing show on the TV."

A porter arrived behind them. "Sorry to interrupt. I have to whisk Mr Tristram away for his X-ray now, ladies."

"It's fine. I think we're done here anyway. All right if I leave you my card?"

"Sure. If I think of anything else, I'll give you a ring."

"You do that. I'll check in on you later, see how you're getting on."

"Look forward to it, Inspector. Hope the information I've given you has helped."

"It has. Thanks. Take care."

Sara and Carla waved at the doctor, and Sara gave him a thumbs-up. They left the ward, stripped off their protective gears and placed them in the bin on the wall. "Well, that was a turn-up for the books. We should get over there and have a chat with Tess, let her know what's been going on and tell her to be cautious."

Carla frowned. "Cautious? I'd be taking her in and offering her protection, judging by his track record."

"Not a bad call, until we track him down. Let's go. I'll stop by and have a word with Colin before we leave."

Colin Rogers was pacing the area close to the notice-board. He glanced their way the second he saw them. "How did you get on, or can't you tell me?"

"Great. We've joined a few dots that were missing. I wanted to give you a pat on the back before we left. You needn't stay around, I think Ethan is going to be all right."

"Are you sure? I don't mind."

"No, you go and enjoy the rest of your day off."

He smiled. "Always a pleasure. I didn't join the force to have days off, ma'am, I joined to assist the public."

"And you've achieved that admirably. Thanks for intervening and, more importantly, for probably saving his life."

"Thank you, ma'am." The constable beamed.

He nodded and clicked his heels together as though he was about to salute but thought better of it. After a moment's hesitation, he set off for the main entrance.

Sara and Carla did the same not long after.

"We need to get over to Tess's house, see what she has to say about all of this, if anything," Sara said.

"Do you think she knows what's going on? She's been a person of interest since day one after all."

"The honest answer is, I don't know, but I intend to find out. If we have to drag her into the station for questioning, then that's what we'll do."

They walked through the hospital and out to the car.

Sara reluctantly paid the extortionate parking fee and threw the ticket onto the dashboard. "Bloody robbing bastards."

Carla laughed. "You're so funny when you're incensed."

"I'm so glad I amuse you." She drove up to the barrier and inserted the ticket into the slot. The barrier lifted, and she threw her ticket back on the dashboard again, tucking it in the corner for safe-keeping, to put through petty cash later. "Let's hope she's in."

"Even if she's been to work, I would think she'd be at home now, sorting out her dinner."

"*If* being the important word in that sentence. Don't forget she's grieving the loss of a loved one."

"Debatable, but yes, you're right. There's only one way we're going to find out."

Sara put her foot down and joined the heavy traffic at the end of the side street. "Bugger, this is not how I planned on spending the next fifteen to twenty minutes of my working day."

"Sod's law when we're in a rush. You're quite within your rights to use your siren."

Sara grinned and did just that. Easing out of the traffic, she overtook a few cars when a gap appeared on the opposite side of the road and paused at the main lights until she thought it was safe to proceed. Tess's home was at least ten minutes from the city centre. Thankfully, the traffic eased on the outskirts of town to a more manageable level, and Sara completed the rest of the journey without the aid of the siren.

She drew up outside and knocked on the door, but it wasn't Tess's door that opened, it was the neighbour's. The woman was standing there eyeing them nervously.

"Thank God you've arrived."

"Has something happened?" Sara asked, her stomach already slipping into a tight knot.

"Yes, I've just got off the phone to the police station, aren't you from there?"

"We are." Sara showed the woman her warrant card and tucked it back into her jacket pocket. "Why did you ring the station?"

"Because I didn't like what I saw."

It was like squeezing the last drop of juice out of a lemon, painstakingly slow, obtaining the answers. "Which was?"

"That man. He took Tess."

CHAPTER 10

"**W**hat? How long ago?"

"Five minutes. I rang the station as soon as I saw him bundle her into the car." She touched her face, and Sara noticed how much her hand shook.

"That must have been very upsetting for you to witness. The more details you can give us at this stage the quicker we'll be able to find her. What car was it?"

Sara was expecting the woman to say a black Range Rover, but she didn't. "A silver Mercedes. It looked like a new car to me. Well, you rarely see old cars on the roads these days, do you?"

"Did you happen to see the numberplate?"

Disappointingly, the woman shook her head. "I didn't, it all happened at the speed of a tornado. One minute Tess was screaming for help, and the next the man had hit her and tossed her in the back of the car. I tried to get to the front door, but my legs aren't that good these days, and I tripped over the mat in the hallway. It's okay, I'm all right, don't make a fuss. I steadied myself and got to the door swiftly, only to see the car take off and turn the corner at the top of the road. Poor Tess. Whatever is this world coming to if someone can show up at your house and kidnap you like that?"

"It's terrible, I agree. Did you get a good look at the man?"

"Let me see. Ah yes, his hair was quite short, brown. He had a rounded face, not fat in the slightest, chubby cheeks my old mum would have said."

"You're doing well. Anything else? What clothes was he wearing?"

"A black or navy-blue hooded sweatshirt. He had it up, to help disguise his features, but I still caught a glimpse of him as he turned to get in the front seat. Jeans as well, the normal dark-blue kind, not the fashionable ones everyone is wearing these days with holes in. These were smart, like new, they were."

"And the car? I don't suppose you noticed the model number?" Sara sensed she was pushing her luck.

"I'm sorry. No, I'm not too bothered about what make and model a car is, all I know is that it was a silver Mercedes. Quickly, you must get after it before he gets too far away with her."

"Don't worry, we'll get an alert actioned. Which direction did they set off in?"

"Down the road."

Sara nodded and smiled. "Okay, you've been really helpful. Thank you."

"Catch him, you can thank me afterwards. That poor woman, I'll pray to keep her safe from harm. You just do your bit and find her before he harms her."

Sara and Carla dashed back to the car.

"We'll do our best," Sara said. "Give the station a call if they return, will you?"

"I'll keep my eye open for them. Good luck." With that, she closed the front door.

"Get onto the station, Carla. See if an alert has been actioned. We don't know if she gave them the details of the car. It sounded as though the make had only just come to her."

"On it now."

Sara took off in the direction the neighbour had pointed out, which she soon discovered led to the main road to Worcester. Carla ended her call.

"Do you think we should keep on this road?" Sara asked.

Carla shrugged. "Maybe. There are several lanes and roads that lead off this one within a few miles. Let's face it, they could be anywhere by now."

Sara slammed on the brakes and lashed out at her thighs. "So bloody near and yet so frigging far." She surprised them both, letting out a scream. "Sorry about that, I feel better now. Shit! As if this day hasn't been long enough already."

"You can't continue through the night again, Sara, you're going to be no use to anyone if you do."

Sara sighed. "Tell me what the alternative is. It's my case, I can't pass it over when something like this happens, I refuse to."

"All right, there's no need for you to shout at me. I was only pointing out the facts. You need your rest like everyone else on the team."

"I know, but going home when we're this close isn't the option, is it? It's getting dark now."

"Yet another aspect we need to consider. My call would be to go back to the station, ensure the patrol cars in the area are on full alert and go from there."

"It doesn't sound right, that's something a defeatist would do, Carla. I'm not one of those, and neither are you."

Carla scratched her left eyebrow. "So what's the alternative?"

"There isn't one as far as I can see. I think we're in for a long night. I hope the team are up for it."

"They will be. I have a feeling most of them regretted missing out on the action last night. Maybe you should contemplate going home for a few hours and leave me running the show instead."

"Nothing against that proposal per se, but I would feel bad walking away now. I can smell the end is near and I wouldn't be able to sleep anyway, so what's the point in deserting the team now?"

"There isn't one, when you put it like that. Maybe you should take the opportunity to grab forty winks in the next couple of hours all the same, you know, to recharge your batteries."

"Don't worry about me, I'll let you know if and when I'm struggling."

"Good. No investigation is worth killing yourself over, Sara Ramsey."

"I agree, partner."

THEY ARRIVED BACK at the station within the next ten minutes. Carla fixed the whole team a coffee, and Sara did the rounds, gathering information from the other team members.

"What do we know about Owen Silver?" Sara asked Christine.

She handed Sara a sheet of A4 paper with the pertinent facts about Owen's active duties out in Afghanistan, and at the end of the page she read that he had been discharged from the army on medical grounds due to a PTSD diagnosis.

"Great, so not to put too fine a point on it, we could be dealing with a ticking time bomb."

Christine chewed her lip and gave a brief nod. "I agree, boss."

"Fuck. What about an address for him, anything there?"

"Nothing so far. We have one on record, but then I checked the electoral roll and found that new people moved into the address around eight months ago."

"Interesting, so where has he been living ever since? At the condemned house where he murdered victim number two?"

"Your guess is as good as mine."

"Okay, Christine. I suppose it's too late to try and find out who his GP is, isn't it?"

"I can ring round the surgeries. Most of them hold an evening surgery until about seven."

"Do that. We need to get the lowdown on how bad his PTSD is and how we should handle it if we catch up with him."

Christine tapped the keyboard and brought up a list of the surgeries in the area. "I'll work through this lot, it shouldn't take me too long."

Sara smiled and patted her on the shoulder. "You're brilliant, thanks, love."

She worked her way around the room and stopped at Craig's desk. "How's it going with the cameras, Craig?"

"Barry and I are doing our best, boss, but the lack of cameras in that specific area is frustrating us."

"I can understand. Stick with it. Same for the ANPRs? You have the make of the car but not the licence number. Have you checked if the car has been reported stolen?"

Both men looked at each other and cringed.

"It doesn't matter," Sara said. "One of you get on that now. Don't take your eye off the ball, gents, I sense we're closing in on him."

"Sorry, boss," Craig replied.

"Don't be sorry, just ensure it doesn't happen again and all will be well within our little bubble." Sara laughed and moved on. She collected her cup and called out, "I'll be in my office. Let me know if anything comes our way." She settled behind her desk and rang Mark. "Sorry, darling, I don't think I'll be coming home anytime soon."

"How come?" He sounded disappointed.

"The murderer has kidnapped a former girlfriend who happens to be the grieving girlfriend of the first victim."

"I think I managed to wrap my head around that. Shit! With the intention of hurting her?"

"Who knows? It's beyond me. Anyway, you don't want to hear about our trials and tribulations. How are you? Did you have a good day?"

"For a change, yes. No major mishaps to cope with. I'm more worried about you, though. It's not good for you to go without sleep two days on the trot, sweetheart."

"I know. It's not in me to up and leave it to the rest of them, Mark. I hope you understand."

"I know it isn't, you're a true professional, but even utter professionals need time to relax and recharge their energy levels. You're not a Duracell bunny, love. Not that I'm nagging you."

She chuckled and smiled at the way he was looking out for her. "I know, I appreciate your concern, but if it's any consolation, the adrenaline is doing a grand job of keeping me going. You're aware what a valuable commodity that is to the body."

"Hmm… let me think about that one. Oh yes, you're right. The decision is yours at the end of the day, Sara, I'm willing to back you either way."

"Thanks, that means a lot. I have to go. I'll check in later, if that's all right?"

"I'd be upset with you if you didn't. I'll snuggle up in front of the fire with Misty instead of you, no great hardship for me."

"You're both lucky. I'm envious. I love you, Mark, don't ever forget that."

"I won't, and ditto."

"Speak later." She ended the call, blowing a kiss down the line, something she rarely did at work.

After downing the rest of her coffee while it was still hot, Sara rang Lorraine's mobile in the hope that she wouldn't be interrupting her on a date. "Hey, are you busy?"

"Never too busy to talk to you. What's up?"

"Don't tell me you're still at work?"

"All right, I won't, but I'd be lying. Are you?"

"Yep. Both mugs, aren't we?"

"Correction, dedicated mugs would be more appropriate. Why are you working so late?"

"I have news for you about the investigation. Do you have time for a quick catch-up?"

"Can you give me two seconds to grab a coffee? The kettle has just boiled, but I never got around to making it. You know what it's like when you get distracted with paperwork."

"Only too well. Go for it, I'll hang on."

"Wait, I can put you on speaker. Yes, I'll do that. Carry on, I'll respond in a tick."

"You're nuts. I don't mind waiting."

"Okay, as you wish, I'll be right back."

Sara started up the computer and picked up a pen, ready to take notes while she waited for it to run through the motions. She typed in *PTSD* and scanned the results, clicking on a link that would give her a brief overview and the symptoms. She had hoped she would learn something new. She didn't.

"Right, I'm back and stocked up with caffeine. What's to do?" Lorraine shouted in her ear.

"Christ, did you think I'd fallen asleep in your absence? You nearly deafened me."

"Sorry, my bad. As you were," Lorraine lowered her voice.

"Okay, here's where we're at. We got called to another crime scene today—"

"What? I don't recall receiving an invite to attend the scene."

"There was no need for you to show up, the victim got away with his life this time."

"Phew, makes a change. What happened?"

"Another soldier. The killer went after him, a revenge attack. The victim had left the pub, and maybe the killer thought he'd had a skinful. Anyway, he hadn't and put up a fight when the killer confronted him. The victim handled himself well with martial art moves."

Lorraine laughed. "Good for him. Did he do any damage to the killer?"

"Not really, not as far as I could tell. The thing is, the victim was able to give us a name for the suspect."

"Bloody hell. See, it's always handy when someone survives an attack."

"Indeed. Turns out he was in the same regiment as the suspect and was able to fill in some details for us."

"Which are?"

"That he was discharged from the army on medical grounds."

"Don't tell me... PTSD, yes?"

"Correct."

"Shit. That's going to be a tough one for you to combat, Sara. You're going to need to be extra cautious and keep your wits about you, if and when you catch up with him."

"I know. I'm researching the condition now. Surprisingly, I've not really had to deal with it in the past. Or maybe I have with certain suspects, and it had yet to be diagnosed. Either way, don't worry, I'll be careful."

"How can I help?"

"Apart from giving me some pointers, I wanted to fill you in on where we're up to with the investigation. If I give you the suspect's name, maybe you can obtain his DNA from the military and compare it to anything your guys have found at the crime scenes over the past week."

"I can do that, no problem. Anything else?"

"Yep, the worst part to all of this is that the suspect—or killer, should I say? Let's call him by the correct terminology."

"Why not? You were saying?"

"It turns out that the girlfriend of Ben Connor, the first victim, used to go out with Owen Silver. Sorry, that's the killer's name."

"Noted down now, thanks. Shit, and you believe that's why the first victim met his maker?"

"Stands to reason, doesn't it? Not only that, he's now sodding abducted her. That's why I'm still at work."

"Fuck. A man teetering on the edge mentally who has kidnapped his former lover. That sounds like a recipe for disaster if ever I heard one."

"You don't say."

"Hey, wait a minute, did you get any rest last night at all? After attending the third crime scene?"

"I didn't go home, if that's what you're asking. I dozed at my desk for a couple of hours."

"Bloody hell, Sara. You need your rest."

"What I *need* is to locate the killer before he ends Tess's life."

"Fuck. I can't see this ending well."

"Not what I wanted to hear, Lorraine."

"Sorry. I take it you have patrol cars out searching for the suspect?"

"Of course. Anyway, it was only my intention to bring you up to date with how things stand, not to badger you for tips how to collar the bastard."

"I feel for you. What about family, have you checked with them? He'd likely been staying at that condemned property, so I doubt if he would have an address he could use, unless he has any family members living close by."

"We're doing the necessary searches now. All we know so far is that he dumped the Range Rover he was using and has picked up another car. We're presuming that's been stolen."

"Seems the most likely scenario. He's doing his very best to outwit you. If he's ex-army, he'll have some cunning traits, so watch your backs."

"Also, he's more than likely got his hands on numerous weapons, judging by the murders he's committed already."

"Absolute nightmare of a situation to find yourself in. I have every faith in you overcoming this, Sara. You're the smartest woman I know, apart from me, of course."

Sara laughed. It felt good to break the tension building up inside. "If you say so. I have doubts if that's true at times, but plodding on. How about you, have you got any plans for this evening? Don't tell me you're going to remain chained to your desk until the early hours?"

"Umm… that was the plan. Thought I'd ring for a Chinese at around ten and then work until about twelve. I'm so far behind with this damned paperwork."

"Lucky Chinese. Be gentle with him, don't go scaring him off like you usually do."

"Ha, you can be such a comedienne at times. Go, let me get on, now that you've disrupted my momentum."

"Ouch, how to make a girl feel guilty with one disapproving sentence."

"You know I love ya. Hey, in all seriousness, take care. Ring me if you think I can be of assistance, and finally, don't work too hard. You're entitled to your time off, babe."

"Pot and kettle comes to mind, and don't nag. I've just had the very same conversation with Mark."

"He's a wise man, I've always liked him. It's a damn shame you got your claws into him before I could."

"Bloody hell. I've heard it all now. He'd be a nervous wreck living with you."

"I tell you what he would be… my sex slave!"

Sara laughed so hard as soon as she hung up she had to run to the ladies' to spend a penny.

"Sara, Sara, are you all right?" Carla shouted a few seconds later after banging on the cubicle door.

"I'm fine. Bursting to spend a penny after Lorraine made me nearly pee myself. That woman genuinely needs to get laid in the foreseeable future. Although I dread her next beau, she'd probably keep him locked in her bedroom for a week or more."

"Oh my. I'm not offering to matchmake again, if that's the case."

"Yeah, maybe we should take a step back from doing that for a while." Sara flushed the loo and joined her partner. She washed her hands, sang happy birthday twice in her head and used the drier.

There was a knock on the outer door. Carla opened it. "What's so urgent that you have to intrude on our privacy, Craig?"

"Sorry, Sarge. We've got a sighting of the Merc."

Sara raced to the door and pushed past Carla. "Where?"

"On the road to Worcester, just outside Hereford. A farmer saw a man and a woman arguing in the car. He said the man was really angry, in the woman's face, and she was in floods of tears. He didn't like the look of it and rang the station to report it as a domestic incident. He said he felt like it was going to turn violent."

"Right, let's get out there. We'll go en masse," Sara began on her way back to the incident room. "I want Christine and Jill to stay here. Will, Barry, Marissa and Craig, I need you all to come with me and Carla. We'll take three cars, in case he makes a run for it. We've got more chance of tracking him down if we split up and take separate routes. Anyhow, we can sort out the finer details at the other end."

"Would it be worth getting an ART organised?" Carla asked.

"We can do it en route. You can drive my car while I make the call. His track record makes him unpredictable. We're going to need all the manpower we can get hold of. I'll have a word with the desk sergeant on the way out, see what men he has available to assist us. Are you ready to go?"

The six of them ran down the stairs, and the other four members of the team rushed out to the cars while Sara and Carla paused for the briefest of moments to see what backup was available.

"Wasn't expecting you to still be on duty, Jeff," Sara said. "We've had a sighting. Any patrols available to help us out?"

"I passed the call on to your team, and the second I did that, I sent two patrol vehicles out to the area, ma'am. I've told them to keep their distance and to hold back until you get out there. And yes, I was certain you'd get on the road ASAP."

"Good man. I knew I could rely on you. We'll keep you abreast of things when we get to the location. Cheers, Jeff."

"Good luck. I'll keep my fingers crossed you catch him and that he doesn't put up a fight."

"I'm going to sign out a Taser all the same." She threw Carla the keys to her car and marched into the armoury to retrieve a Taser from a locker. After signing it out, she waved farewell to Jeff and joined her partner who was sitting in the driver's seat, revving the engine. "Cheeky cow, I haven't been that long. Have the others gone on ahead?"

"Yep, I thought it would be for the best."

"You'd better put your foot down and catch up with them then."

CHAPTER 11

*T*ess was in the front of the Merc with him now. He had bound her hands to prevent her from attempting to grab the handle to escape from the car, or from possibly lashing out at him. He glanced sideways at her. She was sobbing. He had gone over everything with her, assured her that she was his top priority. Emphasised to her all that he'd done so far had been for her. All he craved for in this life now was to hold her in his arms once more. Love her the way she deserved to be loved, not strike if she spoke out against him the way Connor had.

His anger surged once more. It always did when he thought about someone hurting her. She was his. He would do everything he could to keep her happiness at the top of his agenda. Although glancing to his left now, it was breaking him in two to see her so unhappy.

"Tess, I love you. We'll get through this together. I know I could have handled things a bit better, however, my main aim has always been your happiness, nothing has changed in that respect."

Tess sniffled and wiped her tears on the backs of her

bound hands. "Then why am I tied up? Why have you kidnapped me and are holding me hostage? Why, Owen? None of this makes any sense. You say you love me, and yet look at the way you're treating me. Don't I deserve better than this?"

"You do, and once you show me that I can trust you, all of this will change. We'll move on with our lives and begin making plans for the future."

"What future? We don't have one. We broke up, and you've just confessed to killing my boyfriend whom I was very much in love with."

His attention left the road and fell on her tear-stained angry face. "You loved him? But he beat the crap out of you. The evidence is clear to see even though you're doing your best to disguise it under that muck. You know how much I hate you wearing makeup. It's vile, makes you look like a whore."

Tess gasped. "How dare you say you love me then go on to call me a whore, how dare you? Every woman has a right to make herself feel better, wearing makeup does that. Yes, Ben hit me, we had issues we were sorting through together. I seem to recall our relationship was a fraught one and, at times, I felt I had to watch what I said in case you struck out."

"Not once did I hit you. I loved you for the person you were. It was you who gave up on me when I needed you the most."

"I couldn't handle your constant mood swings. Sleeping next to you at night was a trial in itself. The constant night-mares you had to deal with. Yes, I sympathised with you, but I couldn't bring myself to live in that bubble with you any longer."

"You loved me. How could you turn your back on me when I was at my lowest ebb, in need of your understanding and love to see me through the tough times?"

"I feel bad that I walked away, however, I seem to recall myself pleading with you to seek help for your problems. You refused to do it at the time. Then you... raped me. I walked away believing you didn't care, therefore, if you didn't, why should I?"

Ignoring the rape comment, he argued, "You can't walk into a doctor and explain the grim details of what goes on in your head. I tried everything to save our relationship. It was your love that helped me deal with the pain, anguish and anxiety this condition heaps on me." He drew the car to a halt and twisted in his seat to face her. "You were—no, correction—you *are* my life. Without you beside me, I'm nothing."

"And you think holding me hostage is the answer? I *hate* you. I don't love you." She held up her hands bound with rope. "This is so wrong. All you're doing is convincing me I was right ditching you after you raped me. I fell out of love with you for a reason, there was no one else involved in that decision. I sat down one day and forced myself to consider the depth of my feelings for you and I couldn't get any further than thinking that I felt sorry for you. There's no way I could continue being with you when my dominant emotion was sympathy towards you. Any love I had for you had departed. For me, there was no going back. I know your illness wasn't your fault, but it wasn't mine either. There were days when the guilt became unbearable for me. I caught myself standing in the kitchen one day after we had dealt with one of your episodes, holding the blade of a kitchen knife against my wrist. It was sinking to that level that made me take stock of what our relationship had become. Every turning I took mentally to try and ease the situation back-fired. I remember urging you to seek specialist help, but you refused. What could I do? You needed to be able to admit you were plummeting fast before we could overcome what we were dealing with. You always enforced upon me that you could cope with everything life threw at you when you clearly couldn't."

"I'm sorry. But I sought help afterwards, I had to. Losing you was far greater than living in any warzone. Battling to save lives every day and destroying the enemy. Out there, it was your love that saw me through all of that, and then to come home and to be rejected by you... it cut me to shreds."

"I only rejected you after that drunken episode which led to you raping me. So don't turn this on me."

"But I needed you to hold me in your arms and tell me everything was going to be all right."

"I couldn't do that, Owen, because I didn't know if it was true or not. Please, you have to let me go."

"I don't *have to* do anything. I stopped taking orders from people the day I left the army. I did that because I wanted to be with you."

"You didn't leave, they kicked you out."

He turned to face her, and the car swerved. A blast of a horn and Tess screaming forced him to concentrate on the road ahead once more. "Why are you so bitter? At one time we couldn't get enough of each other."

"I'm not bitter. I'm *terrified* of what you're going to do with me. I've already told you that there's no future for us, and here I am, tethered, being abducted. How the hell do you expect me to cope with being in the same car as you? What have I done to deserve you treating me this way? Why kill Ben? And the others you've hinted at killing? Why, Owen, why?" Her voice rose several octaves.

He drove on in silence for the next few minutes, going over the torture and murders he'd committed, and shuddered. *Did I do that? Knowingly? I don't think so. I couldn't have. I don't have it in me to kill people, or do I?*

"Answer me," Tess shouted. "I have a right to know why."

"I did it for you."

"What?" she screeched. "I don't want to hear that I've been the cause of the deaths. How can you sit there and tell me you love me after going out there and taking their lives?"

He pulled the car into a lay-by up ahead and unhooked his seatbelt. "I would do anything I needed to be with you. To have you by my side once more."

"How is that right, Owen, to kill people just to get back in my good books?"

He was lost for words. That thought had never occurred to him while he'd been carrying out the killings. Had it all been for her? If it had, here she was now, rejecting him. He'd screwed up, and he was continuing to do it. What was he doing? How would this situation end? He wished someone would reach out and tell him, because at this point, he didn't know.

CHAPTER 12

"Shit! I wasn't expecting that."

"What?" Carla asked.

They were speeding along the A4103. Carla had succeeded in catching up with the others. They had let her pass once they'd hit the open road and it had been safe to overtake on the winding route.

Sara sighed. "No available Armed Response Teams in the area."

"Double shit! Do we take the risk?"

"We have to. He's holding Tess captive, who knows how that's going to end?"

Carla smacked the steering wheel with her right hand.

"Hey, that's my job," Sara said.

"Sorry. What about the helicopter, can they help us?"

Sara raised a finger. "Good suggestion, I'll get onto control."

Sara requested that the helicopter assist their mission and took a moment to breathe out a relieved sigh. "I hope they're going to find him, what with it being pitch-black now."

"They will. You worry too much."

"I know."

"What are we going to do if we ever catch up with them?"

"What type of question is that?" Sara asked. "We'll deal with the situation when, not if, it arises. We'll need to assess what state of mind he's in before we start shouting the odds at him."

"What if he holds a knife to her throat? How the hell are we going to deal with that?"

"What's up? This isn't like you to put obstacles in our way, Carla, are you all right?"

"Nervous, I suppose."

"Why? Because of the PTSD?"

Carla shrugged. "Possibly. You know when you get a niggling feeling that something is about to go wrong."

"Nope, don't go there. I've yet to have that happen to me. You'll be fine, don't stress about it."

"I suppose what's concerning me is that he has Tess and he's unhinged. I can't see this ending well at all. And another thing, dealing with this in the dark is going to make our job so much harder."

"Don't worry about it. You're guilty of overthinking, and working yourself up into a state isn't going to help either of us. Take a few deep breaths."

Carla didn't respond, but Sara caught her breathing deeply. Her mobile rang, and she took the call. It was the control room telling her that the helicopter was now airborne. "That's brilliant news. We're still on the A4103, no sign of the Mercedes as yet. What we'd appreciate the helo telling us is whether we're heading in the right direction or not. It's the unknown that is dampening our spirits."

"I hear you, ma'am. I'll get the guys to contact you directly once they're in position. It shouldn't take them too long to get there."

"Excellent news. Thanks for the update." Sara ended the

call. "See, you're worrying about nothing, we have great backup to hand. Don't forget we've got the team with us as well."

"Nothing you can say is going to prevent me from feeling this way."

"Then I'll stop trying."

IT WAS another ten minutes before Sara heard from the helicopter pilot. He told her they were approaching the road where it branched off to the Malvern Hills. "I know it. Can you see the car?"

"Not yet. My guess is that's the likely route he'll take. There was nothing on the A4103, heading towards Worcester."

"We'll take the road and see where it leads us. Can you scour the immediate area for us?"

"In the process of doing just that now. I'll get back to you if I find anything. Wait, hold on, I've got a vehicle up ahead. Stay with me. I'm going to get in closer. We're using the thermal image cameras. Yes, I believe we've got the target in our sights."

"Brilliant. The turning is coming up on our right now."

"There's a small wooded area at the top of the hill, on the left. Wait a minute, the car has stopped. I repeat, the vehicle has stopped."

"Roger that. Carla, put your foot down."

The car surged forward, and Sara's head shot back.

"Sorry." Carla cringed beside her. "Ask them what's happening."

"Anything else going on up there?"

"The driver's door has opened. The driver has spotted us. He's watching us. Right, he's darted around the other side of the vehicle. He's got the hostage out of the vehicle now. They're legging it towards the woods. What's your ETA?"

"We don't know, we're halfway up the hill."

"You're around two minutes away then."

"Can you stick with them until we get there?"

"We've got a beam on them, and the thermal camera will do the rest once they start using the trees as shelter."

"Put down that foot of yours and get us there sharpish," Sara ordered.

"It's your car. Don't blame me if I crash into something."

"I'm going to ignore that. Get us there. *Now.*"

Carla put her foot down again, however, this time, Sara was ready for her and stuck her head forward slightly, avoiding a second impact with the headrest.

"It's there. The others are right behind us. Pull up behind the Merc. I'll get the others to surround the car so he can't get away."

Carla parked within inches of the Merc's bumper and switched off the engine. Sara hopped out and directed the other two cars. Within seconds, the Merc was surrounded at the front, back and on the right. The only option open to the suspect would be to go left, but he would have to ram the other cars out of the way first. Sara parked that thought to one side instead of dwelling on it. Cars could be replaced, lives couldn't.

The rest of the team gathered around.

"Right, it's clear what we have to do," Sara said. "We're going to need to split up into couples and handle this the way we did with the car—surround them and flush them out. I'm in contact with the helicopter pilot. He's going to stick with us until we've made the arrest."

"You reckon he's going to stay in the woods, boss?" Craig asked.

"I don't think he's got an option. The second he steps foot

outside with the hostage, the game is up for him, and he knows it. Let's get to work, guys, we're wasting time, and Tess's life is in danger. Barry, glad to see you signed out a Taser, I should have instructed you to do so before we left. I slipped up."

"No problem, boss. I felt it was a necessity, given what he's been up to already."

Sara nodded. "I agree. Don't use it until you feel it's genuinely necessary, and of course, safe to do so. Don't risk hitting Tess. He's bound to use her as a shield, which is why I believe we should surround him, it'll give us the upper hand. So, I want Marissa and Craig to go left, and Barry and Will, you go right. Don't go too wide. I know it's going to be dark in there, but hopefully our eyesight will adjust quickly. If not, then you're going to need to use your torches, but I need you to be aware that's going to give your position away, just bear that in mind."

Sara and Carla led the way into the opening of the woods. The helicopter circling overhead had its beam shining, so that helped to guide them into the dense area. Their colleagues made their move and went left and right as instructed.

"I'm concerned if we're doing the right thing," Carla whispered beside her.

"In what way?"

"If we trap him, how do you think he's likely to react?"

"It's all we have, Carla, unless you can come up with a better alternative?"

Carla's silence was enough to prove to Sara that her partner couldn't, so she pressed on, tentatively avoiding any fallen branches or trunks en route. A few steps ahead she paused, and unfortunately, Carla slapped into the back of her.

"Jesus, you could have warned me."

Sara smirked. "Sorry, I can hear voices ahead. Listen."

They both strained an ear, and Carla nodded. "Yes, I can, too. Definitely a female's voice."

"Okay, we need to get closer. Sounds like they're having a heated discussion." Sara gestured for them to plough ahead.

They moved swiftly for another minute or so and then paused again to listen. The voices could be heard more clearly now.

"Damn," Sara said. "Tess is crying. I think she's trying to talk him around."

"Yeah, he's not having any of it, though, is he?"

"Listening to the tone of his voice, I think he's becoming more and more irate. It's time to make our move. Are you up for this?"

"If you think it's the right time, who am I to argue with you?"

Sara held her hand up, and her partner high-fived her. "We've got this. Together, we'll pull it off. Keep the faith, Carla."

"I'm with you all the way."

Sara took another ten paces or so. The couple came into view several feet ahead of them. By the look of things, Owen had set up camp. He'd started a fire in a clearing away from the trees. Foolish, Sara thought, given their proximity to hundreds of trees in the area.

"I'm going to announce our arrival. Tess sounds stressed."

"I'm not surprised. His voice is taut, full of anxiety. Be careful, Sara."

She squeezed her partner's hand, stood upright from her crouching position and shouted, "Owen Silver, this is the police. You're surrounded. It would be better if you gave yourself up, there are armed police in the vicinity." The last part was stretching the truth slightly with only two Tasers between the team and the lack of any other weapons to aid their mission.

She stepped forward into the clearing, with Carla close behind. Owen immediately grabbed Tess, whose hands were bound. He placed her in front of him. He withdrew a knife from his jacket pocket and held it against her throat.

Shit! He better not kill her. I need to talk him around.

Owen's gaze darted around the immediate area and then focussed on Sara. "Who are you?"

"I'm DI Sara Ramsey, and this is my partner, DS Carla Jameson." Sara's gaze dropped to the terrified Tess who was sobbing. "It's okay, Tess, I'm sure Owen has no intention of hurting you. That's right, isn't it, Owen?"

"I love her. That doesn't mean I won't hurt her if you push me over the edge."

Sara held her hands up. "I have no intention of doing that. Let's chat, Owen, find a way of sorting this out between us, eh?" She raised her voice, hoping that the rest of the team would home in on their location and move forward as planned. Sara had slipped her Taser into her back pocket, still to hand, if she needed to get to it quickly.

"Let's discuss this, Owen. You don't want to do anything rash that you're going to regret later." Sara's gaze connected with Tess's, to reassure her, and then reverted back to Owen's once more.

"I need to get away from here, with Tess. You can arrange that, can't you?"

"Of course. If that's what you want. First, you're going to need to tell me why you killed the three men." Sara hoped that Carla would be sensible enough to record his admission on her phone. She kicked herself for not making the suggestion, nevertheless, trusted her partner to do the right thing.

"I had to."

"Why? I can understand Ben Connor's death. You love

Tess and you thought he wasn't treating her right, that is why you killed him, wasn't it?"

"Yes. Only cowards lay their hands on women. Put them in a room alone with a man and they'd run a mile. Gutless shits!"

"I'm confused by your statement, Owen, you're the one holding a knife to Tess's throat. Doesn't that contradict what you've just said, make you a coward?"

Owen's eyes narrowed, and his grip loosened around Tess's neck. He mumbled something that sounded like an apology. "I didn't mean it, Tess. You know I only want what's best for you."

"Then hand yourself in to the inspector, she's kind. She'll see you right, won't you, Sara?" Tess shouted. She took a step away when Owen released his hold on her completely.

"Yes, we'll come to some agreement, Owen, once you've admitted to the murders of all three victims. Tess only wants what is best for you, don't you, Tess?"

"Yes, that's all I've ever wanted."

In the light emanating from the fire, Owen frowned.

"Then why leave me? We had a good relationship. All this could have been avoided if you had continued to love me. Instead, you let me go, set me free, and I didn't know where to turn to for help. The doctor tried giving me different kinds of medication, none of them helped. If anything, it made me worse."

"Did you discuss that with your doctor, Owen?" Sara asked.

"No. He didn't want to know. Every appointment I ever had with him only lasted two minutes. Patients went in and out of his room like they were on a conveyor belt or something. How can you get to the bottom of a patient's problems and offer solutions when there is no compassion there?"

"Your doctor was wrong to treat you like that. Why didn't you seek help from another doctor?"

"They're all the same at the surgery. No one cares."

"I can get you the help you need, if you'll trust me, Owen."

His eyes narrowed, and his gaze latched on to Sara's. "Bullshit, you're talking the talk but have no intention of following through."

"You're wrong. I have never let anyone down in the past and I have no intention of letting you down either. I will help you, if you'll trust me."

"Why should I? I don't know you from Adam."

"No, but Tess will vouch for me, won't you, Tess?"

"Yes. She's been kind to me. Listened to my perspective. Give her a chance, Owen. What have you got to lose?"

"My sanity. You don't know the pressure that builds in my head daily. The explosions I hear when someone drops something nearby. This disorder has destroyed tougher men than me over the years. I'm doing the best I can to combat the issues, but sometimes it's too much for me to bear, and the need to vent my anger emerges."

"Is that what happened with Ned and Andy?" Sara asked, throwing the other two victims' names out there.

"Yes. Ned used to be my best friend at one stage, but he turned his back on me just like Tess did. Why did you do that, Tess? Ditch me when I needed you the most?"

"I'm sorry. I tried hard to help you, but your refusal to seek professional help at the time made me fear how it was all going to end."

He shrugged. "Not well, has it? All this could and would have been avoided if you had remained by my side. We could have worked things out between us. You could have comforted me on the days I needed it. Instead, you cast me aside when my need was greatest."

"If that's the case, why do you still want to be with me?"

Tess challenged him, finding strength from somewhere deep within.

"Because the love I feel for you overshadows everything else that has gone on in the past. We can change things for the better. I can change, with you beside me."

"How is that possible, Owen? What if we had an argument, how would you react? Go out and kill someone else, punish them for what goes on between us? How is that fair, or right, for that matter?"

"It wouldn't be like that in the future, if you give me the chance."

"But you couldn't guarantee that. Killing these men has become an addiction to you. You go out and kill someone in order to achieve balance in your life. You've just admitted as much. How could we live like that? Under that much stress? If I said one word out of place, you might storm out and take your mood out on someone innocent who happened to be walking down the street. I couldn't live under that cloud of uncertainty."

"But not two minutes ago, you told me you would be willing to give it a try. Did you lie to me?"

Tess turned to face Sara, her gaze darting, seeking help.

Sara cleared her throat. "This is a confusing situation for all concerned. You're holding a knife, Tess still feels threatened. Her words are coming out muddled because of her confusion. Why don't you put her at ease by throwing the knife on the ground?"

"You're trying to trick me. I will not surrender. Tess and I will be leaving this wood together. Get to your feet, Tess. Come here." He went to reach out for her but ended up on the woodland floor, amongst the leaves, fifty thousand volts surging through his body from behind.

"All right, Barry, stop it!" Sara ordered.

Craig and Will ran forward and checked Owen was okay.

The voltage had left him dazed but nothing more than that. Tess took the opportunity to escape, and she ran towards Sara who hugged her and then passed her over to Carla to look after. Sara approached Owen and read him his rights while Craig cuffed his hands behind his back.

"You're all the same. None of you give a toss about the likes of me. I fought for this country, witnessed atrocities you could never envisage, and this is how you treat me. And you believe I'm the one whose mind is in chaos. Take a good look at yourselves and tell me I'm wrong," he shouted.

Craig and Will hoisted him to his feet.

Sara took a step forward and said, "You were the one in the wrong, not seeking the right help to assist you. You're the one who took three innocent lives out of revenge and spite. I'll make sure the families get the justice they deserve, Owen Silver. Take him away."

Sara expected Owen to put up a fight. He didn't. He was led away with his head held low.

She returned to where Carla was comforting Tess. "Are you all right? Did he hurt you?"

"Only my pride. I can't believe I allowed him to take me hostage. How did you know where to find us? I thought we'd never be found."

"Your neighbour saw everything and told us what type of car to look out for and the direction Owen set off in."

"That's a relief. Glad there are still some people willing to speak out these days. I'm so grateful for all you've done for me. What will happen to him now?"

"He'll be assessed by a medical professional before we question him."

"Are you saying he'll get away with the crimes he's committed?"

"Not in the sense you mean. He'll have his day in court.

It'll be down to the professionals to do their job, either defending or prosecuting him."

"Could the defence get him off, though?"

"It's anyone's guess. There's no getting away from the fact that this case has extenuating circumstances. He's not of sound mind, which I believe will probably go in his favour. It's likely that he'll be sentenced and admitted to somewhere along the lines of Broadmoor, a psychiatric hospital. Some people are under the impression it's a bed of roses to be a patient in a place like that. Believe me, it's not."

Tess sighed and nodded. "As long as he's off the streets, I suppose that's what counts. I can't help feeling sorry for him. I would hate to be locked in that head of his. Who knows what dangers are lurking in there?"

"Exactly, which is why he's going to need expert help. Come on, let's get you home. Unless you'd rather stay with a friend or family tonight?"

"I'm fine. Knowing that Owen has been arrested will be a load off my mind."

EPILOGUE

*S*ara was thankful it was her weekend off. She spent most of Saturday morning in bed. Mark dropped into the surgery for a couple of emergency visits from worried owners and then nipped into town to do the shopping. By the time he got back, at around midday, Sara had showered and dressed and was busy in the kitchen fixing lunch for them. She had searched the internet for something appropriate she could make to use up what was left in the fridge and was in the process of putting a crustless quiche in the oven when Mark walked in with four bags of shopping. "Blimey, how many are you intending to feed this weekend?"

"Have you forgotten your dad is coming over tomorrow?"

She cringed. "I had. I was looking forward to spending time with you and Misty, alone. Selfish of me to consider that with Dad's situation."

"Not at all. He's going away for a week, so that will give us quality time together."

"I'd better check with him, see what time he's coming over."

"There's no need. I called him earlier. He'll be here for one o'clock tomorrow. I also invited Lesley. I hope I've done the right thing."

"Killing two birds at once, eh?"

He tapped the side of his nose and leaned in for a kiss. "I'm not daft."

"Far from it. Thank you for always putting me and my family first."

"It's a pleasure, never a chore. How long before lunch is ready?"

"Another twenty minutes or so. Enough time to put this lot away." Sara gestured to the bulging bags at their feet.

"You read my mind. I've bought steak for tonight and a piece of pork for tomorrow."

"Great news. It's Dad's favourite."

He kissed her again, and they restocked the fridge and the cupboards together. He also topped up the wine rack with a few bottles of nice red.

"For tomorrow. Red goes with pork, doesn't it?" he queried.

"I don't know, neither do I care. I dare anyone to complain and tell you differently tomorrow, they'll have me to deal with."

They both laughed.

EVERYTHING WAS in hand the following day, well in advance of her father's and Lesley's arrival at one. Sara trotted upstairs and changed out of her comfortable leisure suit and slipped on a smart pair of trousers and a blouse. Mark always looked smart in whatever he wore. He decided on his new jeans and wore the jumper she had bought him for his recent birthday.

At twelve fifty-five, the doorbell rang. Mark welcomed Lesley into the house.

She entered the kitchen and let out a moan of pleasure. "Smells delicious. Thanks for the invite, sis."

They embraced, and Sara kissed her on the cheek. "Our pleasure. Has Dad said much about his trip away?"

"Oh yes, he's been going through his itinerary all week at every opportunity. He's so excited. The trip will do him the world of good."

"I agree. It'll take the pressure off us, too. What will you do while he's away?"

Lesley smiled. "I've got a few nights booked. I'll be catching up with friends. It'll be a relief to get out again after months of sitting by the phone, expecting a call to come in."

"He does tend to rely on you more than me. Sorry about that, love."

"Don't be. You're far busier at work than I am, he knows that. I don't mind, not really. Can I do anything to help?"

"What about laying the table for me?"

"Not at all." Lesley went to the cutlery drawer and collected what she needed for the four of them.

The doorbell rang again, and Mark answered the door. Her father had arrived. He had an unmistakable laugh, but then a woman's chuckle rang out as well. Sara turned to see her father standing in the doorway with a woman around the same age, dressed in a smart cerise skirt suit and matching coloured handbag over her left shoulder.

Sara wiped her hands on her apron and approached them. Lesley stood beside her.

"Hello, Dad. Who is this?" Sara asked.

"Ah, this is Margaret. I wanted to introduce you all to her before we set off on our new adventure together."

Sara's mouth gaped open. *What? You have a new woman in*

your life and this is how you tell us? "Oh, I see. Nice to meet you, Margaret. Will you be staying for lunch?"

"Hello, you must be Sara." They shook hands. "Umm... I thought I had an invitation to join you."

Sara glanced at a sheepish-looking Mark hovering in the doorway. She raised an eyebrow at her husband. He issued a cheesy grin and hitched up a shoulder.

"Sorry, did I forget to mention it? Lucky I was the one doing the veg for today then, wasn't it?"

Sara laughed. "I thought you'd gone over the top. Sorry, Margaret, it would seem I'm the last to know, as usual."

"Make that two of us," Lesley said snarkily.

Ouch, Lesley isn't going to appreciate being left in the dark.

"It's my fault, girls. I didn't know how to tell you, so I had a quiet word with Mark, and he suggested this was the best option. Don't be mad at me, life is too short."

Sara leaned in and cuddled her father. "Don't be silly. We're fine, aren't we, sis?"

Lesley turned her back and continued laying the table, collecting more cutlery en route.

Sara whispered, "Ignore her, she'll come around, eventually. Welcome to our family, Margaret. Mark can fix you both a drink while I finish cooking the lunch."

"Thank you," Margaret said. "Can I help? I'm a dab hand in the kitchen myself."

"I can vouch for that, her meals have been superb, the ones she's cooked for me," her father piped up.

"Another time maybe. Everything is done and ready to go. Enjoy your drink. Mark, take Dad and Margaret into the lounge."

They all left the kitchen, and Sara wrapped her arm around her sister's shoulder. "Give her a chance, Les. I haven't seen Dad this happy since mum passed away."

"I feel betrayed. He should have told us."

"It's his life, he did what he thought best. Let him enjoy the rest of his life instead of spending it grieving for Mum."

"If you say so."

THE END

THANK you for reading Time To Kill the next book in the series Deadly Passion is available to pre-order here. Deadly Passion

HAVE you read any of my fast paced other crime thrillers yet? Why not try the first book in the DI Sam Cobbs series To Die For.

Or grab the first book in the bestselling, award-winning, Justice series here, Cruel Justice.

OR THE FIRST book in the spin-off Justice Again series, Gone In Seconds.

PERHAPS YOU'D PREFER to try one of my other police procedural series, the DI Kayli Bright series which begins with The Missing Children.

OR MAYBE YOU'D enjoy the DI Sally Parker series set in Norfolk, Wrong Place.

. . .

OR MY GRITTY police procedural starring DI Nelson set in Manchester, Torn Apart.

OR MAYBE YOU'D like to try one of my successful psychological thrillers She's Gone, I KNOW THE TRUTH or Shattered Lives.

KEEP IN TOUCH WITH M A COMLEY

Pick up a FREE novella by signing up to my newsletter today.
https://BookHip.com/WBRTGW

BookBub
www.bookbub.com/authors/m-a-comley

Blog

http://melcomley.blogspot.com

Why not join my special Facebook group to take part in monthly giveaways.

Readers' Group

Made in the USA
Coppell, TX
14 November 2022